Praise for Lan

'Sucker *is remarkable for the emergence of a brave new prose stylist . . . [Lana Citron's] boldness makes for an invigorating read*'
INDEPENDENT

'*Sucker stands out from other urban twenty-something novels for its genuinely witty and original writing*'
LITERARY REVIEW

'*Lively and absorbing . . . Citron's recording eye rarely misses a thing. This novel is a wicked but affectionate satire*'
DAILY TELEGRAPH

'*Citron has a very sharp eye for the rules and manipulations of the sex war. She's idiosyncratic, clever and, like her name, full of zest*'
OBSERVER

'Romance for anti-romantics . . . *Citron's straight-talking style and uncompromising approach to male/female relationships is the ideal antidote if you're schmaltzed up to the eyeballs*'
COSMOPOLITAN

Also by Lana Citron

Sucker

Spilt Milk

Lana Citron

SCRIBNER

TownHouse

London . New York . Sydney . Tokyo . Singapore . Toronto . Dublin

A VIACOM COMPANY

First published in Great Britain by Scribner/TownHouse, 2001
This paperback edition published by Scribner/TownHouse, 2002
An imprint of Simon & Schuster UK Ltd and
TownHouse and CountryHouse Ltd, Dublin
A Viacom Company

1 3 5 7 9 10 8 6 4 2

Simon & Schuster UK Ltd
Africa House
64-78 Kingsway
London WC2B 6AH

Simon & Schuster Australia
Sydney

www.simonsays.co.uk

TownHouse and CountryHouse Ltd
Trinity House
Charleston Road
Ranelagh
Dublin 6
Ireland

A CIP catalogue record for this book is available
from the British Library

ISBN 1-903650-15-1

Typeset in Sabon by SX Composing DTP, Rayleigh, Essex
Printed and bound in Great Britain by
Omnia Books Ltd, Glasgow

for Misha

Acknowledgements

Len, Bongi and Greg for keeping me vertical. Mum and Dad, for your love and support. Judy, Sian, Bethan, Rachel, Anna Maria, Mo and T, Jack B., Martin Fletcher, Hannah Griffiths and Jonny Geller, many thanks to you all.

Wishful Thinking

My arm outstretched, palm upturned and it clutched at nothing. Absolutely nothing. I was chasing a dream when it happened. Unexpectedly and quite unconsciously, it did happen and I did not stop, nor even slow down, but continued in my haste towards a certain future.

It was early evening, weak heat, summer's long left over rays teasing and, if I'm honest, I was warming up to a winter alone. A long dried-out period of oneness. All about me was amber, the dripping gold of an autumn sunset, as if suckling all goodness from the heavens and dragging it down under.

I had a residue of feeling and played with it, humming a happiness that was forced. Mind over matter, though I did not mind too much, and I was thinking how sad it was that some people saved pennies for a rainy day.

I remember having these specific thoughts, as earlier in the afternoon I had passed by an old-time sweetshop: a tooth-rotting Fannie May and it had instantly reminded me of one back home in Dublin. Regan's, long since gone but it was stacked to the beams with chocolate and bull's-eyes, fizzy cola bottles, pineapple drops, lemon sherbets, pink bon-bons, gobstoppers, licorice, indeed all sorts of treat pots, heaped full of sweetness, almost medicinal in arrangement.

As a kid, my father would take me on rare occasions to Regan's Fine Confectionery. Close by his side, with my hand clasped in his, I'd stand mesmerized by the kaleidoscopic selection, my head barely level with the counter. I'd tip my chin upward to watch old Mr Regan, in his beige cardy, with his shaky hands, twist open the jar lids and weigh out a quart of fizzy gumdrops then pour them into a brown paper bag. The expectancy of waiting for the transaction to finish, for it was not uncommon that a conversation would strike up between my father and Mr Regan, and it was all too much to endure before I could succumb to sticky fingers and chewy joy.

Anyhow, when I passed by Fannie May's that image came hurtling back with surprising resonance and I began to play with it. Shelves of labelled jars full of sweet substance changed, to become the dispassionate stockpiling of cold copper security, but why, I decided, stop there and, goading myself on, the image transformed once again, to the stockpiling of kisses.

Ah, I thought, now that is real romance and in my mind's eye I set to, hoarding them. Jars full of kisses, sweet-toothed madness for the excesses which I was loath to waste, which had to be saved at all costs. I tell you the loss of a tooth is merely a bad dream but to fritter away a kiss constitutes something almost catastrophic.

I imagined filling jam jar after jam jar, pouring myself into it, until the vessel was full to overflowing. Each jar dated in red ink, greaseproof paper under the lid, held tight by an elastic band and I'd keep a log book, categorizing each and every lip-pucker with the following criteria: intensity, lasting value, quality and depth of passion. So many different types to account for and I went through them all, counting them out on my nailbitten fingers: raindrop kisses, drizzling on a face to be half caught by an open mouth, soft wetting the side, downpour kisses, jungle wet and warm, desert kisses, parched and dangerous, sun-scorched, wind-burnt or butterfly ones, tongue fluttering. I knew them all and if I didn't I made them up: rapid waterfall kisses, stuttering shy lip-trips, blood-red biting, valley wide, even vomit kisses that splurge out, that shake your insides so. And all bottled up, until eventually every inch of space in my head was taken over by jar upon jar, piled up any which way.

There on the sidewalk compelled to snap out of it and I found myself within yards of a crossing. The late-autumn beams glistened down upon my chapped and swollen mouth, easing the muscles of my face and this is when it happened.

I had walked onward, toward the light, my pace erratic and my mind absorbed, when out of the blue, my right arm darted away from my body and my palm clutched at air, as if physically expecting a stranger palm to join it.

Strange, I thought.

Stranger still, a guy beside me interrupted my train of thought and said, 'That's beautiful man,' as if he had read my mind.

'Get out of my dream space,' I yelled. Nothing is sacred these days.

'Excuse me ma'am?'

Damn, but there's too many freaks. I mean one day soon, someone is going to corner the market in head space. It will become like real estate and you'll eventually end up having to lease, hire or buy it. Whole lifetimes spent in pursuit of controlling your own thoughts, even then regular brainwaves will be intercepted with ads and government propaganda disguised as public information announcements.

'Whoa there little lady. You've lost me,' and his accent, Southern smooth, floated warm from the back of his throat.

Forced to stop, we had reached the corner of the kerb and were waiting for the green light. The one where Superior meets Orleans, near Northside Chicago.

The man stood beside me, had blue-black hair and was sweating profusely. He looked to me like he was on drugs.

'Ma'am, when I said that was beautiful, I was alluding to the sunset.'

He was right, it was blinding and I had to hold my hands over my eyes to shield them from the intensity of the light.

He wore the most outrageous flares with a matching shirt unbuttoned to show off his fake-tanned chest and sparkling medallions. Throwback, I figured, as he winked at me, his mouth curling into a tight-lipped smile. He raised his right eyebrow, tapped the side of his nose and whispered, 'You ain't seen me,' then strode off.

'Whatever,' I sighed, shrugging my shoulders. I was forever attracting that type of incident.

My mother used to say to me, 'There's always one in every crowd,' and for a long time I thought she meant I was number one.

*

Anyhow it was getting nippy, so I wrapped my scarf tight about me, crossed over and found myself outside a gallery. Her name in flashing neon alerted me – 'Kitty R, conceptual artist'. I was taken aback, knew her from when I'd been in New York, hanging out with Jess. Back then, Kitty had taken an instant dislike to me, blaming me, unfairly as far as I was concerned, for ruining her debut show. A messy time in retrospect, but full of curiosity I peered through the gallery glass. The place was heaving, though I managed to spot Kitty, unchanged and still the centre of attention. Contemplating entering, I wondered if she'd recognize me, when the doorman beckoned me approach.

'You wanna come in?' he asked.

'Who me?' I muttered self-consciously.

'No the dude behind you.'

'Sorry,' I mumbled, 'I thought you were referring to me.'

'You gonna stand there all night or come in?'

'Thanks but I should give it a miss.'

'You got another date?'

'Nope.'

'You got some other pressing assignment?'

'No.'

'So what's the problem?'

'I'm lost, was trying to find my way home.'

'Excuse me?'

'It doesn't really matter.'

'You're one weird lady,' he laughed.

Well, as my mother always said, there's one in every crowd. And just as I dispatched that thought, on the very precipice of moving off, I saw him.

Amber-crowned, he stood behind the glass, out of reach, just beyond the doorway.

5

Mothers, and what would you be doing without them?

See I had glimpsed a shock of Titian hair and in the falling dusk it was as if the sun had taken refuge inside. Indulging in some moments of wishful thinking, I remained motionless, lapping up the warmth. If only I could reach out, entwine a lock of light about my finger. Teetering on the threshold, I noticed his attention was focused on another. A conversation struck up and if I'd pressed my ear to the glass I'm certain I would have caught the gist, or perhaps a word or two.

The doorman persisted with his entreaties. 'You sure you don't want to come in?'

I nodded, 'Thanks all the same but I better be going,' and I turned my back to the gallery.

Star Attractions and the Main Event

Manfredi Bracci, stood close to the exit of the gallery. He hadn't planned on being there but Sol insisted.

'Half an hour, that's it, I promise.'

It was Friday and both of them were at a loose end.

His arms dangled awkwardly by his side and he wished Sol would hurry back, having gone to fetch a couple of drinks.

The gallery was packed, people pressed together, one upon another, shoulders rubbed, kisses flying through the air in search of proffered cheeks. Kitty R, the artist, stood close by, flanked on either side by her entourage and Manfredi felt conspicuously in the way. He was looking out for Sol when suddenly she appeared right in front of him. Pushed up against him, their faces almost touching, she trod on his foot.

'Oops,' she blurted as Manfredi shuffled back a step. 'I didn't hurt you, did I?' she asked.

'No, it's fine.' His left toe throbbed in disagreement.

'It's too crowded don't you think? I mean you can't see anything properly.'

'Isn't that a good thing?' Manfredi smiled, giving her the once, twice, three times over.

She frowned. Had he said the wrong thing?

'I'm Kitty's sister,' she grimaced, before moving off abruptly.

*

CALL it intuition, force of will, fate, whatever . . . but the first time I saw him, I just knew . . . instantly understood and realized if there had been any certainty, ever in my life, it was that something would happen between us. What can I say except the feeling fell upon me like a smell, a warm childhood memory or sense of belonging where every tension fled and my whole being surrendered.

Of course I could not trumpet my own arrival, it's not my style and would have been detrimental to the overall cause. In effect, I had to bide my time. It's not often you catch a glimpse of the future. Red the colour of his hair or wispy ginger and his eyes were amber. So I remained the outsider, clocking him before moving on.

Timing as ever crucial . . . probably pushing six as the Angelus had rung. Mother and son bringing a whole country to contemplation and a chord struck in my memory.

Resonating to back then, when my father jumped up, out of his seat, his feet tapping out the rhythm to a song that came flooding through the kitchen on the wireless waves. My father used to dance the jive in our kitchen while I, high in my chair, well fed, having finished spoon travels, banged the instrument as an attentive audience. The radio was blaring with his favourite programme. Seamus Doolin's half-hour of transatlantic hits. We wouldn't miss it for the world. My father's hands upon my mother's hips and she, turned toward the sink, was making the tea.

She shooed him away, 'I've a kettle full of boiling water.' Feet tapping about her, 'Be careful,' she says, as he pulls at her free arm, wanting to twirl her in and out and twirling himself and got in a right old twist.

I was laughing at the pair of them. 'Leave off,' she shrieked as he cavorted once more across the floor. The red lino tiles flecked black and grey. Clicking his fingers and he did wink at me as he rounded on her, for a third time lucky, wanting to surprise her. Humming in tune, he grabbed her by the waist, ready to lift her up. Didn't she only nearly jump out of her skin.

'You great eejit,' she shrieked but he spun her round to face him, her wrist clenched in his hand and he was pressing his cheek up against hers. She succumbed, he succeeded and the pair were dashing back and forth across the lino in time to the tuneful radio. Whooping and laughing, a stranger spectacle I had yet to experience, banging my spoon on the table top, till the last of the notes dispersed and the announcer's voice introduced the next track. They split up, he to bow, she to curtsy and I clapped my appreciation.

'Timing Murrey,' remarked my father. 'It's all about timing.'

See in this game timing is everything and having come so far I was prepared to hover a while in the background and wait.

'KELLY Richards, Kitty R's twin,' observed Sol, in answer to Manfredi's question. 'She's an entertainment lawyer, late twenties, single though dates heavily,' he continued, whilst managing to shovel a handful of chocolate covered raisins down his throat. 'She happens to work for the same law firm as my brother.'

'Really?' and Manfredi was interested.

Sol could have withheld the last piece of information but there was no point. In matters of love, Manfredi always landed on his feet. Women just happened to fall for him and, what's more, make no demands, like commitment. Though loath to admit it, such things never happened to Sol.

'Do you have any idea how long I've ached for that woman?' he moaned aloud.

'Sol, you're engaged to Jocelyne,' replied Manfredi, reminding Sol of his forthcoming nuptials.

Still within his eyeline, Kelly was talking with her sister on the far side of the gallery. Manfredi and Sol, having drained their glasses, found themselves slowly shuntered over to the central exhibit, a large piece of turf hung soil side up, entitled, 'The grass is always greener'.

'Which brother?' asked Manfredi, 'The one having a party next week?'

Sol threw up his eyes in exasperation,

'See? See? Jesus Manfredi what is it with you?'

Manfredi shrugged his shoulders, 'What? Nothing's happened.'

'Yet,' Sol remarked, unable to hide the disdain in his voice.

Of course, Sol was right in his assumption and it was not too long before Manfredi woke to the harsh glare of morning light, creeping over the wooden floor of Kelly's bedroom.

He had gently pursued her, letting her dictate the pace. She spun the usual boy meets girl trail, placed the requisite obstacles in his path to test his worthiness, with last-minute cancellations, an evening with her girlfriends, a chaste night spent at hers, a chaste night spent at his and an afternoon babysitting her brother's kids.

Then, ten weeks on, the chase was over.

'Hey sleepy-head,' Kelly's fingers tousled his curly hair.

'What time is it?'

'6.30 a.m.'

'Christ,' groaned Manfredi.

He blinked, rubbing the sleep from his eyes, watched Kelly move to her dressing table. She smiled in the mirror, framed with photos of friends, while a slightly out-of-focus Manfredi reached over to the sideboard for his glasses.

'You working today?' he asked.

She nodded.

'Any chance of calling in sick?'

She laughed, clasped on her earrings then sprayed some scent upon her neck.

'Can't, I've a client meeting first thing.'

'Important?'

'Fraid so.'

'How about dinner tonight?' He had climbed out of bed and stumbled over one of her teddy bears. An array of soft toys lay at his feet, having been thrown aside the night before.

'I'm supposed to be playing squash,' she answered.

Pulling on a pair of old jeans Manfredi sat back down on the bed. Half looking for his t-shirt, he fumbled through the pile of clothes on the floor.

'You can't leave.' He implored her to stay.

'Why?'

'It's a sign of disrespect. I'll feel used.' Making a feeble effort to pull on his socks, she came over to assure him it wasn't like that at all. Her hands upon his shoulders and lips upon his.

'Not convincing enough,' he insisted and required further reassurance.

*

Kelly arrived at work half an hour late. Manfredi stripped her bed as requested, leaving the sheets in the laundry, then made his way over to his office.

Manfredi shared part of a studio in River West, on the top floor of a converted warehouse, with Sol, who worked as a conference organizer, specializing in the avant garde.

Clasping a *Tribune* under one arm, a grande Americano in one hand and slice of carrot cake in the other, Manfredi was the first to arrive. He sat down at his desk, the paper open in front of him, letting his thoughts meander over the previous evening.

He'd taken Kelly to Spiaggio's, her favourite restaurant and they sat by the huge windows over-looking the beach, trawling through childhood reminiscences to find out what they had in common. All evening they kept the search up, strolling through Lincoln Park, their adolescence, where they thought they were going, where they wanted to be. In the end they decided opposites attract, marking this conclusion with a rose from the flower girl who pinned it neatly to Kelly's coat. He had kissed her, then . . .

'Hey Manfredi. What time do you call this?' Sol, breathless, came bounding in, his face sweat-shiny and wearing trainers.

'You been to the gym?' Manfredi asked, finishing off the last gulp of his coffee before chucking the cup across the studio floor, watching as it tumbled into the can.

'Nah, took the stairs. It's part of my fitness campaign, got to look my best for the approaching big day,' Sol twittered on, flicking open his briefcase before extracting a bag of warm cinnamon buns.

'So was she good?'

Sol had a problem with subtlety. It evaded him and as it was rare for Manfredi to be in so early, he insisted on knowing everything. Manfredi did his best to deflect Sol's questions, claiming he had crucial work to attend to.

Manfredi worked as a translator, copywriter and sometime editor. Originally from Montreal he made good use of his lingual abilities, being the third son of a French maman and fifth of an Italian lecturer.

Folding away his paper, Manfredi clicked on his computer screen to make out he was working. Unperturbed, Sol rallied on, bun after bun, before conceding to the guilt trip.

'And exactly who was it put you two guys together?'

'Your brother.'

'Chuh, the last time I do anything for you, Mr Braccia.'

'Promise?' quipped Manfredi, turning his attention back to his worktop and the tedious translation of his latest commission, a company policy manual. By noon, Manfredi's concentration had waned to near depletion.

The intercompany structure, in relation to office spatial awareness, just didn't grab hold, and suffering a severe spate of yawns, Manfredi found himself tempted by an early afternoon showing. Afternoon movies were his favourite, Monday afternoons even better. The lure of an empty auditorium, sharing the place with, if you were really unlucky, a smattering of old-timers and if you were lucky, a disinterested usher. He grabbed his jacket and asked Sol to take any messages,

'And if Kelly calls?'

'Act human.'

Sol smirked. 'You know you should be a comedian.'

'Tell her I'm at a meeting. An important client meeting.'

'You got it,' Sol pitched, revealing the indelible mark of having worked in a fast-food franchise as a fourteen year old.

Before the lift had shunted to ground level the phone rang, Sol picked it up.

'Hi, is Manfredi there?' a soft feminine voice enquired. Definitely not Kelly, the accent hard to place, but not Chicago.

'No, you just missed him. Can I ask who's calling?' Sol drawled, casually lowering his vocal tones.

'Okay,' she answered, followed by a silence, which had Sol momentarily perplexed.

'So who's calling?'

'Oh just a friend. Listen you wouldn't know where he's gone?'

'See it depends on who I'm speaking to,' flirted Sol.

'Thing is I'm his sister. I just got into town and I want to surprise him.'

'For real? He never told me he had a sister.'

'Actually I'm lying. I'm his half-sister.'

'Really, now that's interesting.'

'Is it?' she replied, 'Or do I detect a hint of charm. Are you trying to come on to me?'

She managed to embarrass him and blushing he blabbed,

'Manfredi's skiving, an afternoon at the flicks, but can I be of any assistance?'

She ignored his offer.

'Which cinema, would you know?'

'Probably the Theatre Royale.'

'Do you think he'll be home later?' she asked.

'Yeah, yeah he will . . . but hey, I think he may have company, if you know what I mean.'

'I understand. By the way, what's your name?'

'Sol.'

'So you're Sol. Manfredi's mentioned you. Listen I better go, but thanks Sol. Thanks for your time.'

'No problemo.'

'Oh Sol, before I forget, don't mention I called, I mean it's meant to be a surprise.' Her voice sweet, like sugar candy.

'Definitely no problemo, ' he promised.

Sol put down the receiver and made a mental note to find out more about Manfredi's half-sister.

It was a Monday, I was on my way to nowhere, having just had a fight with a jumped-up waitress when I suddenly experienced a revelation.

These days everything's sign-posted. A zillion banalities vying for your attention. Buy, drive, drink, eat, wear, live, this, that, the other, the better, best, definitive. Are you losing out? Course you are, as huge neon flashes herald messages of no import. Eyes peeled in case you miss something of any consequence at all. There's so much going on, the most fundamental of things are ignored and it's a wonder anyone has enough time to recognize their own destiny. Immersed in this culture given wholly over to choice, it could, for example and as so happened, become a major effort to purchase a simple coffee.

I was sitting in a café, my eyes skimming the small

ads in search of a job. I attempted to order a white coffee.

The waitress turned on me, 'Do you want whole, low-fat, skim, organic, lactaid, soy or rice?'

I repeated my request, 'A white coffee please.'

'Yeah lady, so do you want whole, low-fat, skim, organic, lactaid, soy or rice?'

Was she doing it on purpose?

'A white coffee,' I snapped. 'Is that too much to ask for?'

'Lady do you have a problem?'

I levelled with her.

'Yeah, I'm looking for a sign and while looking, I was hoping to have a white coffee. Can you get me a white coffee?'

She stared down at me. Instinctively I wiped the back of my hand over my lips, just in case a couple of stray crumbs had stuck to the edge and I was looking a right eejit.

Jeez but these days everything's such an effort and I reckon that's why people are so pushed for time. Too much of it spent on stuff you wouldn't even be able to tell the difference about. During my ripening period, a caffeine high was an afternoon wasted in Bewley's, Grafton Street, over a mug of stewed dishwater. Neither latte, espresso (sure why would you want to be in a hurry?), nor mocha (ah, come on now, you're having me on), or even cappuccino (a cap-a-what?) had a chance against the might of Barry's tea. Why have a coffee when a cuppa would do the trick nicely? Anyhow, next thing I knew the waitress had the manager over, politely asking me to quit the premises.

I relented, 'Okay, okay I'll have my coffee black,' but the manager dug his heels in and pointed me to the exit. I snarled, barked, cocked my leg in a threatening manner, then left.

Blundered on, straight into a freak hailstorm, insisting I take shelter. It was a cold, miserable day. I remember it clearly as I came to christen it 'The Day of The Magpie Incident'.

For years I have been followed aerially by a huge solitary magpie. Wherever I happened to be, I just knew I would find it lurking nearby and sure enough if I looked outside a window it would swoop down and perch on any available ledge or branch or anything that could hold its weight. It just wouldn't let up, wouldn't leave me alone, and though ashamed to admit this, I did attempt to kill it.

I'd open the window and hurl stones in its direction, bought a catapult with which to take aim and fire, even laced bread crumbs with arsenic and liberally scattered them. Many morgue-ish mornings ensued and I carry on my conscience the death of various small animals. However, the magpie persisted with what looked to me like a mocking smile on its beak and, wishing to wipe it, I purchased some clear, super-strength glue. Next day I woke to hear a dawn chorus of agony. Drew back the curtain to reveal a row of blackbirds lined up like Hasidic Jews, beaks battering against the glass as they rocked to and fro in their effort to flee. Happily some did manage to get away but only by leaving their claws behind.

The ingenuity of that magpie astounded me. I didn't understand. It eventually became a constant feature in my life, reaching the stage where I had to indulge my suspicions and salute it every morning.

When I came to Chicago I thought I was at last free.

It did not appear, not once, not twice, not ever. I even taunted myself, 'Cooey,' I shouted, hoping to coax it down from some branch on high but it never materialized. Until that morning when I was wandering the streets in search of a sign, a job and a decent coffee.

Was it really too much to ask for, a simple white coffee? I yelped inwardly, head hung low as the hail spat down on me and, finding cover, I took from out of my satchel a stack of letters. Since my arrival I'd applied for quite a few job positions. Couple of hundred or so and already I'd received a heap of replies and all of them stating that, though I was by far the best candidate, unfortunately, owing to the abuses of simony, nepotism, despotism and circumstance, the job was no longer available. I cursed my luck and tore those letters into a million pieces before scattering them to the wind. It was a wretched day, cold, wet and windy and every piece of paper fell into place at my feet so that I was surrounded by rejection.

Beneath an El-track, protected by the beige steel girders, I waited for the hail to ease, looked across the street and there suspended on a wire was the magpie.

Only this time it was not alone, beside it was another. Two magpies and they flew down from the wire to where I was standing. I moved into the shadows, just in case they should be scared off and they seemed to dance at my feet. Then, as they soared into my past, I noticed on the ground two feathers, one the colour of night and the other the colour of innocence. I picked these up and put them in the pocket of my bag, knowing then that things could only get better.

The hail ceased and the skies cleared. I felt an

overpowering need to share the moment and decided to call a friend. Then, picking up from where I was, I set off down the street looking for a place in which to dry.

ALONE in the Theatre Royale, Manfredi sat in the very centre seat of the central aisle, his damp coat draped over the chair by his side, waiting for the main feature to commence.

The once-plush, red velvet curtain rose as a tanned Adonis struck a golden gong, sounding the beginning, just as the doors at the back of the auditorium pushed heavy open and she appeared in the gap as if heralded by her own light. Late and she too alone and the door closed to snuff her out.

In the darkness of the cinema, the projectionist's light angled above, she stumbled forward. Manfredi could hear her blind curses, damn, shit, fuck, hissed out, like she'd stubbed her toe, continuing mole-like to the seat directly in front of his.

She stood there a moment blocking his view. He thought of saying something but decided instead to cough softly, in case she had failed to notice his presence.

'Sorry, I'll just be a second,' she whispered in reply, then unravelled her scarf, unbuttoned her coat, unwrapped the cloth from off her body and removed her hat to sit, sniff, shuffle.

First hint of a sniff not caught in a tissue was always a bad sign in the cinema and Manfredi considered moving. He'd give her two minutes, if she hadn't settled by then, he'd say something. On guard he waited, mentally marking the time, one minute, three minutes, seven minutes passed and just as he was about to relax again, she took Manfredi by surprise. Her head swivelled back towards his, at the exact moment the leading lady stepped into frame. Just as the heroine came sauntering along a kerbside, in a loose summer floral dress, her neck twisted round to face Manfredi and she declared in a boastful whisper,

'I have a dress just like that.'

'Pardon?' he asked, caught offguard.

'I said I have a dress just like that,'and she offered him some popcorn.

Manfredi declined, his gaze diverted away from the screen. Her presence had disturbed him, agitating him. The film dialogue was replaced in volume by her furtive munching from a cardboard carton of popcorn and fizzy cola straw-sipping, leading his concentration to veer from the plot to what idiotic thing she might do next. She had altered his mood, the dreamy state he'd been in dissipated, the languorous calm of the early morning left him. Manfredi tapped her on the shoulder,

'Look, I'm trying to watch the movie,' and to make the point crystal clear, he put his finger to his closed lips.

She turned her back to him smartish, sinking low in her seat and though he let it go, he was sure he heard her mutter, 'Jerk,' before finally and thankfully, shutting up.

Eventually the background reclaimed Manfredi's focus and soon enough, she in front faded.

To Manfredi's relief not another sound emanated from her and by the end of the movie he'd forgotten she existed. As the last of the credits scratched across the surface of the screen, she rose hurriedly, grabbed

her hat and coat and scuttled off up the aisles.
Manfredi dawdled a while, unfolding his still damp
coat, then noticed she had forgotten her scarf. It had
fallen over the back of her seat and lay at his feet,
crumpled. He picked it up and followed her shadow
out of the auditorium to the foyer. Her scarf, a rich
burnt burgundy in colour, was soft and velvety, like
liquid in his hands. Instinctively he lifted it toward his
face, detecting a delicate scent of wild roses and fresh
autumn rain. The foyer was deserted and, rushing
outside, Manfredi stood in front of the Theatre Royale,
his head twisting from the left to the right. Squinting
hard he caught sight of her scurrying forward into the
late afternoon, before she turned and disappeared
down a trunk-lined street, bereft of leaves, of cover.

Raising the scarf again he took in a deep breath. He
liked the smell, thought of Kelly dabbing on her
perfume and wondered if he could trace this scent.

In two minds whether to keep it or hand it into lost
property, he was convinced by the deserted foyer and
box office. After all it was only a scarf, he could always
leave it back in the cinema in a couple of days. He
stuffed it in the pocket of his coat, before making his
way back to his apartment.

I STOOD in the Weiner Circle by Lincoln Park, trying to
steal some heat from off the steambins of the dog carts.
Joe was screaming at the bemused tourists, 'What do
you want. Come on, come on, what do want?', holding
a hot dog in one hand and bun in the other.

The tourists were Japanese and wanted to take his
picture. He charged them ten bucks. I told them, if they
wanted they could take mine for five, but they didn't.

Cold, damp and miserable, I was berating myself for losing my scarf and sensing I was on the verge of a lip-quiver, changed tack, urging myself to pull myself together. After all it was only a scarf.

Actually, it was probably my most prized possession. I'd picked it up the previous summer, off a stall at a New Age/One World/Countless Dimensions Festival. It stood out amidst the usual tat of wind chimes and joss sticks and fluttered at me. The stall owner, an old American Indian, with a weather-beaten face, leant forward and clasped my hand.

'This scarf,' he claimed in a rasping voice, 'it's magical.'

Dipped in the blood of ten generations, the scarf linked all his descendants. I wondered why he was getting rid of it. He told me he'd been cursed by succumbing to a wayward life of loose women and crude alcohol. The only way left to redeem himself was to forgo all his earthly goods. In white man's terms I guessed he was facing bankruptcy and having to sell off the family china. He scoffed at my callous assumptions and point-blankly refused to bargain. In the end I paid full price; besides, he guaranteed me good luck and said, if unsatisfied, I could have a full refund.

Bloody scarf, worst of all I knew exactly where I'd left it. It must have fallen over the back of the seat in the cinema and lay by the feet of that jerk. Him hushing me up. Sure I've as much right as any to enjoy an afternoon movie but now I regretted having wasted my time, for my neck ached. How my neck ached, plus I'd seen the film a thousand times before.

It was one of those stories of fated passion. The actress, with translucent yet dark qualities and icy cold stares, so obviously bubbling under with a volcanic passion, cries out to her mother, a looming presence in the background,

'Mama, from the moment I saw him, I knew I loved him, that (*pause*) . . . I could never live without him.'

And she can't.

See, the actress is driven mad with passion for the hero, but he, mesmerized, has fallen into the claws of some femme fatale. Innocently he carries about him a secret code, which the femme fatale must appropriate for a vicious mafia boss. So when the actress discovers she is not the only woman in his life, she is cut to, cut through, cut up and the bathwater goes a dark luscious red.

Red the colour of shame. Red as the lipstick smeared over the femme fatale's lips as, simultaneously, she kisses the hero then her own life away. Toodle-pip waves the mafia boss, dropping the 'e' on the femme's second name by having one of his henchmen bludgeon her to death.

As for the hero? Well he escapes. Tumbling into his clothes, he flies down the fire escape, tripping on the kerb, just as a woman in a loose floral dress saunters by . . .

'You must have seen it Joe, it's a classic,' I panted, racing my own words and winning.

Joe was refusing to make smalltalk or maybe he really didn't care.

'Yeah, yeah, life is a movie. Now quit bugging me and let me make a few dollars.'

I could take a hint.

'Fuck you Joe. Loser.'

It seemed I'd been hanging down in the circle for hours, treading the mill, trying to figure a way out. For the past ten weeks I'd been staying with Dora, an old acquaintance, her hospitality dependent on my selling these gawd-awful pin roses to love-struck couples. I cursed Dickens and derided Shaw for romanticizing such positions. For every rose sold, a hundred refusals, a thousand snubs, a million humiliations. Okay, I was exaggerating, but my nose had begun to run and I could feel a cold brewing.

Dora was like a sister to me, a pain in the butt, though she meant well. She had previously helped me out of a sticky situation and I felt obliged to stay with her. It wasn't as if we were buddy buddies, she just insisted I owed her big time which I did; besides there was no point splitting until I got sorted. She was in a continual fix, a complete mess, had gone to the edge and abseiled over. There's no two ways about it but I linked Dora with those solitary magpie days.

Kow-towed by a sense of guilt it was up to me to keep her buoyant, at the least to ease her pain. I knew if I returned to hers penniless and with a full basket of roses, she'd throw a fit but love shied from the damp and cold. My search for sheltering lovers yielded nothing and in the end I had to throw a wish at the star-streaked heavens. Oh for a small pot of gold to fall into my hands, nothing too extravagant, just enough to cover the next few days . . . and then I saw it.

An opportune moment and I could not resist, for I had spied a golden glint. It winked at me and offered up its snout. Flirting like a young hussy on a promise.

Are you dancing, he queries.

Are you asking, she replies.

Spinning a trail right before his eyes, and dazzling him so, he wouldn't know what day of the week it was.

A small pot of gold. Sure it was mine for the taking.

Easy does it and I checked for obvious signs of owner-
ship. Not a soul in sight for I lost religion a long while
back. The fact was some idiot had dropped their wallet
right in my path.

Can you believe it?

Finders keepers. I chucked the wilting roses behind a
bush and headed back to Dora's.

MANFREDI slipped his key in the lock of his 14th-floor
apartment, kicking the door ajar. He'd stopped by the
deli on his way back from the cinema and dazed by the
choice his arms were now laden with groceries. He
placed the bags on the small kitchen bar, opening the
refrigerator to pull out a carton of cranberry juice
which he gulped back slowly, checking his machine for
messages. Disappointed Kelly hadn't left one he
grabbed the remote from off the counter, jumped down
on to his sofa, and began flicking through the TV
channels. He checked the time, late already, and
suspected she must have decided to play squash.
Sprawling himself out over the divan, he sank back
content to watch a *Ren and Stimpy* classic he'd seen
before. Then, just as he reached that point of comfort,
when the whole body begins to relax, the phone
bleated its inevitable interruption. Kelly, he guessed,
rising up to wonder where he'd left the goddamn
handset.

Manfredi's apartment, comfortably messy, was
small and cramped. The refuge of a recognized
hoarder. Every inch of space accounted for, even the
floor was given over to piles of comics, magazines, a
music stand, bicycle parts, skates, looking like the
cupboards had randomly spewed out their insides. A

large rectangular aquarium, full of dying pot-plants, balanced precariously on the broken shelf of a built-in unit crammed with books, an 8mm projector, old LPs and vast CD collection. In the opposite corner stood a 1950s broken black and white TV set with a lava lamp aglow on top, a bass guitar leant up against it.

Manfredi scanned the room, kicking over papers and plunged his hand beneath a tatty maroon leather armchair, rescued several years ago from the garbage men. He cursed the place, as the answerphone kicked in, thinking it time to consider a bigger apartment or a cleaning lady. Familiar thoughts and he probably would do both, eventually, but for the view of the city staring him in the face, the fourth wall of the apartment being a floor-to-ceiling window.

He'd found the place with an old girlfriend, a set designer. A couple of her illustrations still hung on the wall. They had lived together for almost six months before she ran off with an actor. It had been because of her Manfredi had left Montreal, pursuing her to Chicago. Twenty-three at the time and having just left college, he had followed her on a whim, five years back.

Outside it was dark, the caller ringing off just as Manfredi found the handset plonked so obviously in the fruit bowl.

He dialled Kelly straight back.

'Hey what's up?'

'Manfredi?' She sounded surprised. 'I was hoping you'd call. I've lost my Psion. All my numbers, absolutely everyone I know is on it.'

'You didn't just call?'

'No. Hey, d'you want me to call by?'

Manfredi recalled her previous visit. He'd excused

the mess as merely interim, due to his cleaning lady being on vacation, but that was six weeks ago. He glanced across at the grocery bags, slumped on the counter and thought it best he went round to hers.

'What about the game of squash?'

'My friend had to cancel. It's been one of those days.'

Manfredi showered quickly, dressed, grabbed the groceries and caught a cab over to Kelly's.

DRIFTING off, my head upon the pillow shouldering thoughts. The day rewinding in tune with rapid shallow breaths and not a fluffy sheep in sight. I ached to go deep but the exhalations kept catching and, inflated with stale air, I wondered if I'd ever float away, hoist sails and un-anchor.

Beset by a sinking feeling I bobbed on a sea of injustice.

I'd come back to the flea pit to encounter Dora, licking her lips like the whore she was, waiting for her tip. Tall and gangly, she was a sorry sight. Her hair all matted, her dark skin pockmarked, each vein invaded and desperate thin. I handed over the money which brought a huge smile to her face and, rolling her tongue, she told me she was rrrreaally happy to see me, that she loved me, was sorry ... I didn't want to hear. The sooner I was out of there, the better.

I swear I hadn't planned on staying with Dora. I really thought I'd left that murky episode behind but there she was at Union Station calling out my name, claiming it was some type of Karmic 'thang' that we met up in such circumstances. I steadied myself, determined I wasn't going to flinch, I wasn't going to give in.

'Good to see you Dora, but honestly there's no need. I have a place in mind already.' In mind, if not in actual existence but it was worth a try. I was feeling positive.

Avoiding Dora would have been tricky, for she'd turned a few on my behalf.

'Don't be so stupid, you're staying with me. It'll be like the good old days,' she issued the order.

The good old days? My memory failed me.

I whimpered, she wrapped her arms around me in a stranglehold and ushered me out of the station.

'You sure are a strange fish,' she said, offering me a cigarette. I refused, had managed to give up.

'Mind if I do?' she asked and I shook my head.

'You have a match?' and I shook my head.

'So what's in your hand dummy?' she laughed like a jackass, her insides seeming to echo a rattle.

Tightly held was my ticket out of a predicament I was on the verge of stepping into, like a brand new pair of trainers with a million grooves on the sole side about to slam-slide on some fresh steamy turd.

It was one of those flick-boxes of matches you get free in bars and restaurants. A guy I'd run into had given it to me, I wanted to keep it for personal reasons but Dora grabbed it off me. A match made in heaven and I winced as she pulled each one away from the base, tried to light it and failed. We walked fifty yards, burnt sticks strewn in an ad hoc trail, one strike left, lit, watching as she sucked in the smoke and the end of the cigarette glowed orange.

Chucking away the empty box, containing my emergency numbers, she dragged me further astray, yelping like an excited pup.

'Yeah, are we gonna have fun or what?'

What?

Then she leant right up into my face, to blow smoke in my eyes, 'Boy oh boy, were we upset when you just took off that time.'

It had been a case of itchy feet. I had my reasons, not that she'd have understood.

Twinkle toes and I'd had to disappear.

'Yep, we were real peeved.'

A smoked-out blow-in to the Windy City and I whimpered again, vowed I'd stay with Dora a month at the most. Her place turned out to be real basic, a one-and-a-half roomed apartment over a crummy bar called Dino's. I slept in the half room, originally a walk-in closet, which meant I had to sleep in a foetal position and also accounted for the fact that it didn't have a window. A soiled mattress covered the entire floor space preventing the door from closing properly but it beat sleeping on the sofa. Dora inevitably had friends over.

Exactly ten weeks on and I'd been keeping count, notching them up against the skirting board. Soon as I got myself a job with a future, I'd be off.

I'd thrown my stuff in the room, plodded back through to the kitchen and found Dora soaking in a glow of narcotic bliss. I left her concentrating on the homeward journey of a cockroach, back into the clock of the oven, where all its pals had been cooked to a slow but untimely death. I took a shower to warm my aching bones then collapsed on to the mattress. Pulling the blankets up over me, the best thing about the room was the fluorescent stars stuck to the ceiling.

Looking up, they reminded me of my father.

On the darkening of every night, my pillowed head and drowsy, I would turn to him to whisper,

How far can a kiss be thrown
As far as the stars
And further
All the way to America.

Star-spangled country, the land of dreams. My father told me it was the land of dreams. Sleepy head, to slumber there, to follow in his footsteps and shroud myself in a blanket of stars.

He would kiss me on my forehead, cheeks and the tip of my nose.

For every star is a captured kiss.

And as I fell into a one-way dream to morning, I began thinking back to when I first arrived in the States. That time when I was old enough but younger than I am now. My skin at its mock thickest and I flew on a plane to New York City.

I carried with me a large grey suitcase packed full of inevitabilities. Hopes to travel light had been thwarted, my history forbade it and kept me in a constant state of remembrance, certain I was forgetting something.

To then touch down, at the back of a queue, with a crick in my neck, and when I reached the top, an immigration officer took my passport off me and examined the photo inside. He looked me in the eye and enquired in a rather officious drone,

'Are you who you purport to be?'

'Do I have a choice?' The thought had never even occurred.

'Pardon?'

'Well do you see anyone else being me?' I enquired innocently.

'Ma'am I see thousands of people every day.'

'Presumably . . . So?'

'Meaning?'

'Need I say more.'

'I get you,' he answered. 'Business or pleasure?'

I paused, then with a residue of pompous adolescence, quipped,

'I'm hoping to make it my business to have as pleasurable a time as possible.'

He cringed and asked where I planned on staying.

'You don't happen to know of anywhere yourself?'

He groaned incredulous. 'Are you kidding me?'

'Far from it.' I explained: 'See I sort of envisaged hailing a cab and being driven all over the city by some non-English-speaking immigrant, neither of us having a clue where we were headed, whether I had a piece of paper with an address scrawled on it or not. So I thought why bother.'

This made him laugh and I guess he warmed to me.

He stamped my passport and, passing it back, said I could stay with him if I liked. Informing me his shift finished in a couple of hours, he told me to grab a coffee down the hall and wait for him there. My gatekeeper to the here and now. To my future. A sorry state the land of my birth, stuck in the past, doused in alcohol and bleary-eyed, I'd flicked a match at it and walked away.

Young and full of dreams, I set forth, yearned to become a fraction of myself. In this place of vast plains and opportunity I could rewrite my history. A Coca-Cola kid, I was the future generation.

Then to be suddenly drenched in an atmosphere of transition over a cool drink. Waiting and I drank it in for it made me thirsty. See I had arrived at a point I

31

could take off from. Oh promising land, my insides erupting at the prospect and I let out a low long moan. It sounded like 'mother'. I'd almost forgotten. The kiosk opposite sold tacky souvenirs, last-minute memories, an 'I thought of you' to scribble down those first impressions.

Dear Mother,

Just a quick note to tell you all is well, the sky is still above me and my feet are on the ground. There's a woman sitting opposite, who looks a bit like you and I was struck by the impossible thought you may have followed me here. She's wearing a cherry-coloured coat and came right up to ask what the time was.

Mother I feel elated though strangely invisible. Everything is so huge here, it quite puts me in the shade and the people, I swear, I never saw such a selection. It's a contained chaos, a sort of Babel, thing is I haven't even left the airport yet. Promise to let you know how things develop, once they do.

Sincerely yours,
Murrey

PS. I think cherry is a colour that would strongly suit.

'Yo crazy lady, what you doing?'
'Writing a letter.'

The immigration officer somehow looked taller sat in the perspex examining booth. Unfortunately when he came to meet me, he was only five-foot-two and drenched in nauseous cheap aftershave. I asked if he'd been an actor in any 1970s cop dramas but he claimed he hadn't been born till '75.

His name was Drucker Floyd Jnr.

Drucker Floyd Jnr drank coffee, sweetened, five lumps, that's real sweet lady. He watched over people day-in day-out and lived with his sister and her kids in some lost suburbia on the outskirts of town. We drove over an hour to get there. The walls were paper thin and I could hear his sister snore. Drucker lay beside me, had pushed me to the edge of the bed, his arm flung across me so I didn't fall out, his duvet was stripy, blue and grey and smelt of too many nights of sleep. His room smelt. There was a chipped mirror on the wall, a small desk and plastic chair. He collected nail clippings and hardened pieces of skin which he put in a plastic ashtray, by the side of his bed.

Drucker told me he loved me.

'Baby I think I'm in love with you.'

'For real?'

He said he liked my attitude, my openness, warned me that people in New York were hard. Everyone wanted something, it was a city of ulterior motives.

'Don't trust no one baby, not even yourself.'

I reproached him for being so cynical, the world was a good place. I pointed to myself. There I was, my first night in the New World, with a place to lay my head and a good man who loved me.

Drucker reckoned I was naive.

But said I could stay with him as long as I liked.

I left the next morning. I mean why go to New York City if you're going to stay out in the 'burbs?

Actually I didn't have a choice.

Drucker's sister said he was going to be real cut up if he got home and I wasn't there.

I'd stumbled into the kitchen, sleepy eyed. She was

slicing a piece of bread and raised the knife so I could see it clearly.

Very clearly.

Though I didn't quite get the point, so she pushed the blade right under my chin.

Ouch.

She said, 'That sure is a large bag lady, you must have been planning on staying a while.'

'As long as it takes,' I replied and in the circumstances, suggested she keep it.

She said, 'Contents will do just fine.'

Heck what did I want with all that stuff weighing me down?

She seemed pleased by this gesture and lowered the weapon.

'Anything else?' I asked her.

'I'll tell Drucker you'll be back later this evening.' She smiled, winking at me.

'Whatever,' I mumbled watching as she counted out the money from my wallet.

In the hazy half-light of the morning I could see her counting out the money. Dora down on all fours and her hand in my knickers. It was late, I must have overslept.

'Dora what the fuck are you doing?' If I'd been a Vietcong, I'd have ripped her to shreds.

'Just taking what's mine.'

Fuck sakes, and I told her she could have it all. Stupid bitch must have been spying on me. See she usually went for my purse but I got wise and started trimming down the contents to five or ten bucks, stuffing the rest in what I presumed was a safe place. She'd obviously cottoned on.

'You disgust me,' I yelled.

I mean did she think I wouldn't notice? My knickers, rolled into a ball, hidden beneath the pillow.

She let out a pathetic laugh, like it was something friends just did, before scrambling off. I jumped up, pulled on some clothes and left. It really was time to move out.

Outside the rain fell like horse piss, the wind licking my neck, reminding me of my lost scarf. I headed towards the local diner, Al's, as it had free papers and as much coffee as you could drink for two dollars. I'd work my way down through the announcements while I woke up properly.

It wasn't until he sat down that he noticed her, alone, a paper discarded at her side, her hands wrapped round a coffee.

Manfredi was a regular at Al's since he'd first set up in Chicago. An initial place of refuge after he'd been ditched by his ex-girlfriend. Amy had left him a note, a thousand apologies and informed him she had fallen in love with someone else, no one he knew. To her credit; she left a month's rent so as not to inconvenience him, she hadn't meant to hurt him. It wasn't supposed to end like this. Words learnt by heart and recited on daily strolls, as Manfredi tried to work her out of his system. Till they lost all meaning and he got his bearings. Then at last, the final flush came and went and it was about this time Manfredi noticed the café with its low-hung lamps, like some long-lost Hopper. The interior was old fashioned with formica tables, the back wall mirrored, waitresses with name badges and worn thin smiles. Grubby colours and digestible fare, subdued atmosphere but real, Al's had no pretensions.

With the damp cloying, Manfredi pushed open the door of the diner. He'd arranged to meet Kelly for a quick lunch.

He glanced over at Debra, the manageress, who was a good friend of his. She stood, sidled up beside a customer, her notepad resting on her right hip, a pen perched behind her ear, beneath scraggly bleached hair and black rings, under kohl-smudged eyes. Tipping his chin up at her, Manfredi saw his favoured booth was empty and went to sit down. With his elbows leant on the table he was undecided whether he should order straight away or wait for Kelly to appear when four rapid-fire sneezes disrupted his concentration and he raised his eyes to the mirror placed along the wall above and looked upward.

There, three tables from him was a hat, perched upon a folded coat, upon the radiator. The windows of the cafe were sheathed in condensation and he could see wafts of steam rising where her rain-drenched coat lay. She blew her nose in a serviette, then bent forward, writing something on a piece of paper, raising her head every so often to catch a stranger look, though failing to notice his.

It had to be her, the girl from the cinema. Her hands clenched around the mug, her mouth lowered to its rim and Manfredi kept his eyes raised as she gulped the contents down. Twisting in her seat she beckoned to a passing waitress with the refill pot. Momentarily Debra stepped into view, to pour the dark liquid into her mug. Once more she picked up her pen and fixed her eyes straight ahead in search of a thought. Then as

if struck by one, her gaze lifted and was caught by a
further reflection, of himself, staring straight at her,
three places forward.

Both faced the same direction and for a split second
were caught within one another's sight.

Manfredi watched as her lips repostured, the ends
turning upward, then part and she stuck her tongue out
at him. Unsure of her intent, Manfredi lowered his eyes
abruptly.

She had definitely noticed him, although he couldn't
be sure she'd recognized him from the cinema.

'She's cute, huh.'

Debra appeared beside Manfredi to take his order.

'What d'you mean?'

'Someone whose appearance is attractive, that kind
of thing.'

Manfredi smirked.

'Know anything about her?'

'Been in a couple of times, guess she's new to the
area.'

Again he felt his eyes drawn up and disagreed with
Debra. No, not so much cute, but quietly beautiful.
Not seekingly so, not the type that demands attention
and Manfredi liked that, to be drawn into someone.
Her look enticing with perhaps a hint of sadness,
though he could not be sure and she looked young or
youngish, younger than him, though he could not put
a specific age on her.

Reaching inside her bag for an envelope, he watched
as she carefully folded the page in two and eased the
letter in. Hastily she wrote out the address, slowly
licking the gum seal and it struck Manfredi she did so
almost provocatively, slowly running her tongue along
the paper edge. So slowly and the thought occurred

that she may have been doing it for his benefit, that she had noticed him. This belied by what he perceived as a smidgen of self-consciousness, aware she was under surveillance.

Suddenly shifting angle, she wiped the back of her hand across her mouth, as if her previous movement was distasteful and smacking her lips together, she checked her watch, gathered her belongings and asked the waitress for her bill.

Kelly arrived and swung down into the pew. Manfredi leant forward to kiss her, but their timing askew resulted in the tip of his nose clashing with her forehead. He pulled back, the pain making his eyes smart, his palm clasped over his nostrils.

'Shit,' he winced. It stung like hell.

'I'll get some ice.'

'No really Kelly, it's fine.'

His protestations ignored as Kelly was already on her way over to Debra. Manfredi hated being made a fuss of.

She arrived back with a plate of ice and began rubbing the end of his nose. Looking round she raised her brows at him, 'Bit dismal don't you think?'

He should have known it wasn't Kelly's type of place and suggested somewhere else. She said it didn't matter, she only had twenty minutes before having to dash off again. Glancing over the menu, Kelly ordered a small green salad and when it came, left it untouched on the plate, while Manfredi tucked into his usual pastrami on rye. Exactly twenty minutes later she left.

He dawdled over a latte, the urgency of his job not pressing or inspiring enough to have him run back to the studio. At any rate, not worth getting wet for and he lingered a while watching the sidewalk traffic caught in a downpour.

The rain began to ease as the steaming sun wrestled for meteorological predominance. Manfredi checked the sky, guessing it would be a short-lived battle, for dark clouds lay brooding in the distance. Pulling on his coat he went to pay the check. Then on his way out, bent forward to tie untangled laces, he spotted a lone black glove, beneath the radiator, in the third booth back from where he had been sitting. Exactly where the girl from the cinema had been sitting and walking forward, he reached under to pick it up.

Was she setting a trail? As if, and he handed it to Debra, just in case she should come back for it.

THERE I was, bang in the middle of writing a letter to my mother when he seized my attention. He was wearing a pale grey jumper, sat down in the back booth, his back broad, blue scarf round his neck. He didn't seem to notice me and I sat watching him, three booths back, pondering the possibility. Red hair, amber eyes, sallow skin and freckled. I asked one of the waitresses who he was. She said he was a regular.

I thought she said irregular.

'What do you mean?'

'Comes in here all the time.'

Interesting.

Then I caught his eye over a coffee, didn't want to let go.

Staring right at me, making me feel self-conscious. A dreamy quality fell upon me and immediately I linked it to the magpie incident and the two feathers that lay at the bottom of my bag. Requiring no further confirmation I was convinced this was a love at first sight scenario. Albeit one-sided.

It's not so unusual, to stumble head over heels and fall. Sure I'd spent my life tripping up. My mother said I was born with two left feet. Resurrecting myself to a toddling three foot, grazed and dazed, she said I'd stigmata on my knees. Stigmatized more like, the kids in the playground pointing and whispering and ... heavenly father who art in heaven, watching over me for sure. And I gave thanks for there I was falling again, at the first sight of love.

See it happens more than is noticed.

Actually, it has happened to me quite a bit.

Take the episode with Jess for example.

I pressed up against Jess the second night of my arrival in Manhattan. Seeing as Drucker's sister had left me for broke, the most sensible thing to do was walk towards the bright lights of the big city. It felt like I was in a movie and I remember I was wearing my favourite summer floral dress, so I didn't have to wait too long for a pick-up.

Bagless and feeling unhindered, I wandered aimless, naivety and youth my trusty angels. Or more like, I trip-hip-hopped upon a club and managed to blag my way in with just enough ignorant bravado. On the door a female security guard stood checking over the entrees. She was dressed in sweats and from the moment I saw her I just knew I'd feel safe in her hands.

Walking towards her I threw my up arms, to ease her access to me and as her palms ran down over my body, I declared,

'You've got to look harder than that. Please.'

And further I exhorted, 'It's your moral duty and perhaps even a pleasure.'

Suspiciously she looked me over, 'You've some neck.' True it is swannish, pale and apt to catch cold.

Anyhow her first compliment given, received and then she escorted me into the ladies to finish the job off properly in one of the cubicles. Pulling a small packet from out of her pocket and a fifty-dollar bill we started sniffing one another out. She licked her finger, dipped it into the small parcel of white powder and ran it over my moistened lips.

'Ah joy,' I exclaimed.

She gave me a quizzical look,

'My name's Jess.'

'Jess is okay by me,' I answered, shrugging my shoulders while her tongue flicked at the sides of my mouth. She left me dishevelled but certain I was in with a chance. 'I'll wait for you,' I said. 'Till your shift ends.'

'Okay kid,' and she flared her nostrils at me as I zipped up her jacket.

Straight away I moved into Jess's apartment in Tribeca. It was tiny but we did it out real nice. To begin with, neither of us was there much, that summer spent partying, clubbing and exploring the city. For the first time I felt free to lose myself. I was anyone, everyone and no one cared. Sure I could hardly hear myself think, what with the incessant noise of the place. I reckon that's why Americans talk so loud. I used to put it down to them being a vocally ostentatious nation but it has more to do with the sounds of wailing ambulances, police sirens and pounding horns.

New York, a city of continuous motion, sensory overdrive and straight off I found a job in a café with an in-house bakery, which was cool as I like the smell of fresh bread. Or rather hot, cause it meant when winter struck I never once felt the cold. But it was fine and I never looked back, my upright neck perpendicular to my shoulders.

I really did fall in love with Jess. She was strong and protective, not conventionally pretty but her body was amazing. I could see all the muscles under her skin, the definition of her ribs, her taut rolling stomach. She worked out a lot and it was kinda like she had manufactured a type of physical transparency.

She had a huge motorbike, a black Yamaha V-Max, and patiently she taught me how to ride it. We used to zoom around the city at dawn, eating yesterday's buns brought home from the bakery.

I remember one morning, riding the Staten Island ferry, holding hands watching out for the dawn, back and forth across the river, talking about our dreams when Jess asked,

'Murrey what do you really want to be?'

'A dancer.'

'You serious?'

'I dunno, maybe, yeah.'

'You ever been to dancing school?'

'No.'

'You had private lessons then?'

'Dad taught me.'

'He was a pro, right?'

'No but he was very good.'

She laughed in my face. 'Murrey if you ask me . . . you've already missed the boat.' But I hadn't, asked her that is, and that was the first difference between us I noticed. Jess was always jumping to conclusions, from dreams to reality. What you want to do and what you do, are two entirely different things but already she was up on her Jessie pulpit, preaching at me. If you want fame, you got to work for it, you got to bust your gut, sweat like a pig or some such words. She told me she had a friend called Leroy and he was a contempory dancer.

'Leroy the king,' I commented, hoping to change the subject.

'You what?'

'It means, the king,' I explained.

'You're real smart aren't you?'

I liked to think I was smart enough, no Einstein but no Alec either. After school, my mother pinned all her hopes on me going to university so I failed my final exams on purpose.

Jess said, 'Education isn't worth piss-shit.'

'That's cause you're a bouncer,' I replied.

She glared at me and a shiver ran down my spine.

'Murrey if you wanna survive in this world, you got to learn some basic things.'

Cupping her hands around my face, Jess told me she'd soon knock some sense into me.

I snapped back to reality, coffee in Al's, playing eye-tag in the mirror till I spotted an interloper. She came rushing into the diner, all tall, slim, attractive, blonde and practically perfect. My vision altered, for she was heading toward him in a corporate sexy manner. A definite career type, probably had wall-to-wall meetings so she never had to feel at a loose end. The type of person with a job and a future. Already I resented her. Then she sat down opposite my admirer and tore his gaze away from mine. Stole him and if I hadn't witnessed it myself, I wouldn't have believed it. Ruining our moment and feeling like a fool, I knew, of course, they were a couple, she was his girlfriend.

My mother used to tell me I was for the birds.
Cuckoo.
Oh Mr Magpie you teaser you.
I paid the bill and hastily left Al's, ill prepared to face the continuing onslaught of the elements and search for employment. Passing a mailbox I took out the letter I'd just written to my mother and popped it in. Maybe she was right all along. They usually are. I mean what was I thinking, falling for a face in a mirror? A mere reflection? It's like a bird banging its beak against what it assumes is a stranger cause it can't even recognize its own self.

I set forth consoling myself with the memory of what happened with Jess, the aforementioned great first love of mine.

I remember exactly when things started to warp between us. I was so wrapped up in her it was a while before I lowered the blanket to take a peek at what was going on. It all began when she discovered a letter I'd written to my mother.

Dear Mom,

It's Sunday morning and I'm lying in bed. Jess has gone to the gym but has promised to buy the papers on her way back. There is bowl of hot milky chocolate at my side, the real stuff not the powdered rubbish and two jelly donuts I've been picking at. We're meant to be going to a friend's performance-art piece this evening but I'm not sure I want to. The last one consisted of four naked women, one menstruating, one masturbating and the others at toilet. Mother in your day this type of thing would never have happened. So much the better for it, I mean really, get a grip. The piece was entitled 'A Woman's Right to Function', and described as a contemporary anarchic reaction to the integral. Mother it sickened me so, I joined in. Vomiting up my condemnation but some of the women got a bit iffy because a) I hadn't taken my clothes off and b) it was a profit-share do. Jess went crazy, she wouldn't talk to me for three days and said I was way out of order, stuck in a long-gone era of anal respectability. I took this as a compliment but bought her flowers anyhow. She has put them on the bedroom dresser and I am looking at them now.

Two hours later . . . Oops left this letter lying round, Jess read it and is now in the foulest of moods, she has gone out with a girl who wants to be the next Warhol. Her name's Kitty R and Jess reckons she is an amazing talent. Anyhow I'm going to cook Jess a beautiful dinner, clean the flat till it shines so I'll send this on the way to the deli.

Hope you are happy and your blood pressure pills are working.

Love and kisses . . . . all the way from America.

Murrey

PS. Sorry it's taken so long to write. A year, I can't believe it, by the way I think you may have been right about doing resits, ah well maybe when I come back I'll consider it.

PPS. Since I've been here I haven't once bumped into anyone I know, never had to pretend not to notice them, no embarrassing avoidances. Such a relief, you know what I mean, although I have been mugged twice.

Back home, you couldn't step out without someone taking down your particulars, walking into the same faces day-in day-out, but here, no one gave a hoot who the hell you where. If I lay down on the pavement I'd be walked on, so I had to keep moving. Maybe I was getting tired or feeling a little vulnerable but it was about this time I realized Jess had changed.

She seemed to have changed or not changed enough, or maybe it was I who had changed; anyhow it was definitely time to move on.

I remember one evening when she arrived home drunk. I was sat in the kitchen with Renata, a sweet Hispanic girl I was friendly with at work. We had both put on weight since being at the bakery and were in the middle of having a moan. I'd just removed my top to show her my extending belly when Jess burst in. She was meant to have been working. A tension descended immediately.

'Am I disturbing something here?'

Well what could I say?

Jess stood behind me, her elbows on my shoulders, her chin grinding into the top of my head, looking suspiciously at Renata clambering back into her clothes.

I tried to level with her.

'Look Jess there's just no point weighing yourself fully clothed, you'd never get an accurate measure.'

'Bullshit,' she sneered.

'No really it's true.'

She wasn't interested, come to think of it facts weren't her forte, being brawny as opposed to brainy.

Anyhow her chin was digging in, so I offered to make tea but Renata said she had to be going and Jess offered to show her out. The stifling weight of expectancy, the slam of the door and back Jess marched demanding explanations then landed me one with her fist.

Right in the mouth.

So brutish and possessive.

Of course I deserved it. I raised my hands to my face and started balling my eyes out, boo-hoo, hoo, begging her forgiveness. She slapped me round a little more, harder, harder, calling me everything under the sun, calling me a parasite, a blood-sucking, fucking parasite.

Afterward we ended up making love, the best we had made in ages.

But it wasn't the first time, sure I'd met plenty of people over the year and Jess was one to talk. She could never keep her hands to herself, I swear I was blue in the face from her.

'Love hurts,' she'd say, so I guess it must have been love. My panda eyes, her terms of endurement. And it got me thinking, I mean, if I was a parasite, then she, by God, was my sporocyst. A yellow-bellied fuck-up. She was a phase I was going through.

You know the type, leading you towards a pained comfort zone. Pretending they are something when they clearly aren't. Right from the start there was something fishy about it, the situation just smelt bad. To think the whole relationship had been nourished on, sustained by, stale bread. I should have realized this from the off.

A love at first sight or the first sight of love?

Whatever, for in the long run it was irrelevant, and in a blink it was all over.

One bright and breezy morning off I took, with Jess's helmet and her bike and I began to ride south.

On the south side of a Chicago street, the rain ceased and I came to a stand-still, wondering if Jess had ever forgiven me. She'd loved that bike more than anything, much more than me. See I had wanted to teach her a lesson, stupid unfaithful bitch, so she wouldn't forget me in a hurry. The white winter sun shone directly in my eyes and I turned my head to be arrested by a sign in a restaurant window, which read, 'Are you looking for a job with a future?'

Yes, I answered, that was exactly what I was looking for and I tried to adopt an aura of assertiveness. I read on.

'Turn waiting to your advantage, make money from it. We're looking for smart young waiters/resses. All interested apply within.'

It was one of those cool-looking cafés, all chrome and clean, exuding attitude, the antipathy of Al's. I stuck my head round the door, took a gulp and hoped my body would follow suit.

The manageress sat me down at a corner table, poured an espresso into a thimble then charged me three dollars.

The first question put to me was who I had worked with.

I asked her.

'How do you mean?'

'You know, what big Hollywood names have you worked alongside?'

'None.'

'Aw that's too bad. Been in any sitcoms?'

'No.'

'Shows, ads, walk-on parts?'

I could tell she wasn't exactly warming to me.

'Ain't you ever done nothin' in the business, ain't you even studying performing arts?'

I was in a school play once, I must have been about six. We were performing the nativity and I got to play a bleating sheep that spluttered on the doll in the crib. It was a walky-talky doll with a pull string. I'd always wanted one of them.

Anyhow in the assembly hall with all the parents watching, my finger somehow became entwined and as I was baa-ing away, the wise men came knocking on the door and the little baby Jesus squawked,

'I can sing for you.'

'I cry real tears.'

'You are my best friend.'

Of course the audience laughed uproariously, they thought it so funny and I blushed fluorescent to show it was me while at the same time I came over all sheepish.

The manageress was clearly unimpressed.

Guess I should have told her my life was my art, every situation a performance. These days people lap that kind of bullshit up, should have said I was inter-active in the true meaning of the word.

'I'm not a hard woman.' She leant over me. 'But haven't you even got a famous friend, or someone, who knows someone in the movie world?'

My negative replies drove her to exasperation.

'Shit girl ain't you got no aspirations?'

At that exact moment? . . .To have an ice-pick at hand and stab her repeatedly so that she died a slow and painful death.

I thanked the manageress for her time and left. No doubt Dora would be expecting me back at the Weiner circle and I headed off making my way toward the park.

It was the weekend and Manfredi, unassuming and by that very virtue noticeable, carried a Saturday *Tribune* under his arm, appearing as if he was on his way to or from somewhere. He was in fact merely going from morning to afternoon, having had no prior intention to be where he was, at that time, when it happened, again.

He had left Kelly at Oak Street to go shopping with her friends. Saturdays were, she had warned him, sacrosanct, to be spent with the girls. He understood, had already disrupted her schedule by staying over every night of the week with her. Striding along, Manfredi had no desire but to wander haphazardly, wherever the day would take him. He fell in step behind a couple. The pair was a human wall of waddling obesity. Pavement-pounding windbreakers and he cowered behind as they led him to his destiny. They turned sharply inward and he found himself rummaging through books at the Aspidistra, North Clark St.

He left the pair to search out a couple of titles he'd been meaning to purchase, ended up with both and was on his way out when he saw *her*, again.

The girl from the cinema, from Al's, was on her way in and Manfredi stalled like he had forgotten something and turned back on himself.

She bore the cold on her face and as the heat of the shop struck, she melted as if perspiring and stopped to wipe the back of her hand over the end of her dripping nose. A red leather satchel hung, draped over her left shoulder as a child's, allowing both arms freedom of movement and her hat, stuffed in one pocket of her coat, was tumbling out over the edge. A perfect excuse, Manfredi thought, to nudge her gently on the shoulder and point to its potential loss.

At the least, a possibility.

He kept a comfortable distance, as she strolled past desks heaped with books, watching to see which one would tempt her to pull up.

She wandered over to the European section, to browse through the titles, seemingly looking for a particular one. An attendant nearby drew her attention and upon her request directed her to the other side of the desk. She rushed toward the empty space, as if perhaps someone else might get there before her and then spotting the book, *Anatomy of a Kiss*, picked up a copy, carefully running her fingers over its cover. Standing close to the display, she held the book open in her left hand, just above the small pile. Then unashamedly and without the slightest hesitation, her right hand eased the top copy off the stack and slipped it into the front pocket of her satchel, while her eyes fixed on the pages in front of her, tipping them low to hide those other movements.

Replacing the newly spine-creased book, she glanced to the right, to the left and then skirted the borders of the stand, randomly going from one title to the next before moving on to the magazine rack. In tow, Manfredi was close enough to notice her reading an astrological horoscope piece.

He could have intervened, there and then, wedged between the racks and the desk, as a fictitious character blessed by such fortuitous moments and wondered if she was aware they kept crossing one another's paths.

Her hair, black, was pulled off her face and tied up at the back, her skin pale and eyes watery. She had painted her lips a deep red and prominent, they looked set to take over her face.

He wanted to do something, say something and undecided, though definitely dithering the moment fizzled. She had turned quickly and was making her way towards the exit.

Manfredi followed, frog in throat, croak now or never.

'Excuse me, ma'am,' beaten to her by an interloper.

Words seemingly unheard, unflinching, she was merely feet from the door.

'Excuse me, ma'am,' the attendant cried, rushing up behind her and elbowing Manfredi out of the way.

Her pace quickened, nervy like and bumping straight into an arm-linked couple, she trashed through them, hardly courteous, on the threshold, to be in a matter of seconds out of sight, had not the attendant managed to step across her pathway.

Shadowing her, Manfredi watched on.

'Let go of me,' she, manhandled, blurted with a blaze of embarrassment streaking across her face.

The attendant's words blocked her getaway, 'Excuse me, ma'am, but this fell out of your pocket,' and he handed over her hat.

'Oh,' she smiled surprised, 'Oh that's really kind. Th-thanks,' relieved she stammered, stuck it on her head and strode forward.

Manfredi walked out alongside her, in step.

'I saw you,' he ventured.

'Pardon?' she answered, folding her arms across the satchel.

'In the bookshop.'

To be caught offguard, to which she, the once-more threatened (for godsake, it was only a book), snarled, 'If you don't fuck off right now I'm going to scream,' in terms most defined and city literate.

Perhaps not the best opener, concluded Manfredi.

She stopped abruptly and turned to face him, her mouth open in high-pitch readiness.

Quick salvage to get back on the sidewalk to Redemption or so Manfredi hoped.

'No I mean . . . before in the Theatre Royale, I found your scarf.'

'What?'

An attempt to clarify fate.

'The Theatre Royale, downtown, and then in Al's earlier this week I saw you . . .'

She looked at him agog.

'Are you following me?' Her eyes sneering mischievously at him.

'No I just happened to see you,' he explained in all honesty.

'Are you a jerk?' she asked testing his reaction.

'No . . . it's just,' Manfredi faltered, 'Can I start again?'

Please, with his big boy smile all helpless.

At last it dawned on her: 'The film, I get you. You know I can't wait till winter passes, I keep losing these damn things.'

Recognition in the nick of, and Manfredi laughed.

'Manfredi,' he said holding out his hand, as if it would explain everything.

'Murrey,' she replied, pausing to add, 'Did you

really see me in the book shop?'

He nodded.

'I mean taking the book?'

'Yeah.'

'Damn I must be slipping up.'

THAT day in the store when I stole the book, it was a Saturday. I was so cold and hungry, had hoped to gorge myself on words and nourish my soul. I'd been searching the whole of the city for a written explanation of my situation, or, at least, a gripping yarn to spin about me as a shield. There I was, running in and out of bookstores, just so I could steal an experience or two. I had in my possession a whole library of counterfeit emotion, of *Héloise and Abélard, Antony and Cleopatra, Romeo and Juliet, Tristan and Iseult,* you get the picture. In my neediness, I had developed a love of literature and would read and reread encounters, memorizing every moment, then take them on as if they were my own.

Literally on the lookout for affection, I went to the Aspidistra, this being my intention, nothing more, nothing less. My sole purpose and that's how it happened, more or less, except he, my secret fancy, exceeded such intentions and to my surprise appeared in person.

Again. And I couldn't quite believe it.

Again, absorbed in his own world, he failed even to glance in my direction. So I bided my time and left the shop to wait till he had made his purchase, allowing me to brush by him on his exit. He stood by the cashiers, paid for a couple of books and then on his way out I made my entrance.

Showing off in the bookstore, I knew he was watching me, half-hidden behind the book stand, silent and there I was, stealing stories. Still he didn't approach, he stood back and I racked my brains, stalled by the magazines to read my stars, check out if I was doing the right thing. Hoping to be caught out, by him, not the attendant, my heart in my mouth as I shoved my hat back on.

And he kept his distance and forward I marched, back into the cold, to be tapped on the shoulder,

'I saw you.'

He said those very words.

Ah but I saw you first.

He told me the woman in Al's was an acquaintance and asked if I had time for a coffee, I wanted to say yes. I was on my way to a job interview. I was late and if I continued to dilly-dally, I was done for. He didn't have a pen. I didn't have a pen, the bus came trundling up the road and I knew I was going to have to run for it.

'See you in Al's,' I yelled.

The doors shut and the bus shuntered forward. Waving goodbye before we had even started.

Mr Manfredi with red-hued curly hair that flopped untidily about his face, angular, amber eyes, sallow skin and lips full . . . to cat and mouse, then leave an impression forming.

Already I wanted to know more.

So happy I was dancing on the tops of tables, well that's my justification. In reality I was savouring another part of the American experience: table-top dancing at the Pyscho Nag 11, where I played auditionee and Jake Johnson played, 'Born in the

USA'. I mean how can you dance sexy to that?

After various gyrations I undid my bra and the guy's eyes nearly popped out of his head.

'Jeez, well would you look at those!'

'Nice aren't they?' I cooed, shaking them in his face.

'Nice!!! What fucking century are you in girl?'

'Excuse me?'

'I mean what do you call those things?'

'Diddies, boobies, breasts, tits, mammary glands. Sir I'm surprised by your reaction,' and I truly was.

He gawped at me, like I was some strange mutant. 'It's just I ain't seen the real thing for eons. It's like they look raw or undercooked.'

Every dancer at Pyscho Nag had fakers, pumped-up solid flesh balloons.

He considered me a risk. 'I'm not sure our clientele will go for this kind of stuff. It's too specialized, although we do have a few perverts.'

He was so freaked out by my breasts, he wondered if it would be okay to touch them.

I wasn't bothered either way. 'Sure, okay.'

We went into his office and he sat me down on his lap.

'Murrey I'll need to take a few more personal details.'

He asked me a load of sexual stuff, like which position I favoured, what was my strangest experience, had I ever had a threesome. I answered as diligently as possible and he listened intently.

Eventually he pushed me off his knee, saying he had cramp and as it was getting nippy I started putting my clothes back on. This is when things got a bit hairy.

Jake stood in front of me and asked if I was an undergraduate.

'Pardon?'

'Well all our girls here are doing it to pay their way through college,' he explained matter of factly.

'You're not serious?' The disbelief in my tone obvious, my voice rising with contempt. 'You gotta be having me on.'

He told me get real.

I did as bid.

'Oh course it makes perfect sense now, a flesh-led market ecomony due to the global dumbing down of society whereby everything is sexualized.'

'Yeah, they bring a certain intelligence to the job.'

'Is that so?'

'Sure and it's real good for publicity, in this day and age you don't just need to be pretty to make your way in the world.'

'Are you saying I need some academic qualification?'

'The punters lap it up, our top lady is a nuclear physicist. So what about yourself?'

'Biochemistry.'

'Really, see that's too bad, we already have three bio-chemists. Now if you'd studied the arts, say the romantic languages, that would have fallen in your favour. You've a neat body and you're cute in a babydoll way.'

'Oh well.' I rose to go. I'd had enough.

'Hey lady wait, there is an alternative.'

'What?'

'Well you could do it voluntarily. There's always that option.'

'How do you mean?'

He explained the situation. 'Every Tuesday we have an open session. A friend of mine is a therapist and he always has a load of ladies who do it as a form of therapy.'

'I'm not that fucked-up though.'

'Hey this is profound stuff, don't scoff, the ladies get a real thrill out of it, it's an empowering process.'

'What like the tables are turning?'

'Sure that's good. Yeah so Tuesday is free trial night, with a load of crazies, come down, we'll try you out.'

I couldn't believe it. Truth was I was finding it near impossible to get a decent job. Nothing too fancy mind, just something that would keep me mentally stimulated. Believe me it was getting to the stage where thievery was fast becoming my only viable option and no longer a party-piece.

So I stole a book, no big deal, nothing in comparison to what I'd taken in the past.

Some people would call me a nymphomaniac, I mean kleptomaniac, maybe just a clapped-out maniac. Anyhow as regards the art of thievery, all I know I learnt from Dog. He would take me on thievery expeditions, where I'd play Oliver to his Artful Dodger.

Another fine mess I got myself into on the trail of the lonesome star.

Dog.

He was human. In form. Two inches taller than me with long dirty brown tangled hair. It was a statement of sorts, but not much of one. He was like that, full of proclamations, usually empty. I mistook it as a strength, a protective layer of thick skin.

He found me unconscious on the highway. On Route 56 Jess's bastard bike died a hazardous death. It reared its last, threw me fifteen feet into a ditch and I landed in his bed. He was stitching up my leg when I woke. I still have the scar, it winds around my knee like a fossilized caterpillar that never quite made the cocoon stage though I remain hopeful that maybe one of these days a butterfly will burst forth. Anyhow Dog lived in a trailer park, in a tin camper van and when I raised my eyelids open he asked,

'What's cooking kid?'

Haphazardly riding for a good few weeks had left me listless, nothing of interest swooping down to ground me. This situation seemed convenient, at least it fell in my lap and what with my wounded leg there really was no point in moving. Sure the bike was a complete right-off but there was a certain romance about being under the star-streaked heavens. Dog appeared nice enough, chatting away like he hadn't had human contact for an age. He hadn't and the reality was he couldn't do enough for me. His hospitality so far reaching, like all the way inside me, that I had to tell him to take it easy, as my leg was real sore and I was scared the stitches would burst. After he finished, he rolled off me and lit up a smoke. Exhaling slowly he whispered, 'You're an angel sent from heaven.'

'Actually New York,' I answered.

To which he replied, 'You must think I'm a fool,' and accused me of lying.

So early on in our relationship I should have taken note, it didn't bode well.

'Dog I'm telling the truth.'

'Liar. That's no New York accent.'

I came clean, told him I was from the land of little green men.

'Wow I knew you were special.' He made some

weird guttural sound. 'So Murrey exactly which stratosphere?'

'Oh God,' I muttered, not sure where he was coming from. 'Look Dog, what you probably want to know is where I'm headed?'

He told me to forget it. 'You've lost me Murrey.'

'That makes the two of us.' I yawned, closing my eyes cause he was blowing smoke in them.

Dog didn't move about much, he preferred to travel static and existed on a herbal dimension. His place was a shiny shrine to auras, crystals, floating spirits and any manner of metaphysical matter. He could only connect with things invisible to the human eye. My own paleness had him baying.

Vehement in his howlings he would turn his snout up at the moon and declare, 'Reach out and touch, feel the force, man, woman, dog, it doesn't matter. Yeah . . . Dog, even I can do it.'

I began to dispute his philosophy,

'Dog we can't live off fresh air.'

We had run out of supplies and were attempting self-sufficiency, but in that desolate place and in our condition even the desert snakes were too quick off the mark. We were wasted and starving and that's when Dog brought me on my first excursion.

He drove an old red Buick truck and once every month or so we'd go in search of gas stations or small-town grocery stores to stock up on provisions.

'Taking what's ours by right,' proclaimed Dog, for he felt he was owed, like his very birth had incurred some heavy debt on society. 'I ain't got time for big-town bullshit, it's a prison out there,' which in a sense was true, as the last time he'd been 'out there' was serving time in George Town Correctional Institution.

We'd pick on places run by kids or old folks. Kids were easy prey, never gave chase and one even helped us load up. Most of them were looking after the store on behalf of their pops or uncle, who was in the Big Town on business or drinking with the boys. The kids were bored and I guess they thought we were slightly exciting; on the run or desperadoes and we'd play that role so they wouldn't be disappointed.

'Murrey you should always carry one of these,' advised Dog, presenting me with a handgun. It weighed heavier than it looked, shiny steel and petite. I begged him to steal me a pair of white-tasselled cowgirl boots, then I really could act the part, but he said I didn't have go method. So I pretended to be bad, got quite good at it, even got to use the gun a couple of times. I'd always aim over the target's head, leaving bullet dents on the wall. I suggested it could be our signature, our mark of defiance, but Dog had a thing about traces of evidence. Anyhow I got too big for my metaphoric boots and on one occasion missed.

Look it was Dog's fault.

He happened to be in the wrong place at the wrong time. Thing was he wouldn't get out of my way. I pulled the trigger and grazed his arm pretty bad. The storekeeper hysterical (with laughter), told me I could take what I wanted. Dog, on the other hand, wasn't so amused. Totally livid, he refused to speak to me for three days, even though I reminded him he was lucky to be alive.

My lucky dogstar.

*

A few weeks further down the line, we chanced upon a scam with an old lady. I'd go in and pick out all the groceries needed, walk up to the cash desk, like I was going to pay and then Dog would appear. Scaring the wits out of the two of us, he'd help himself to her old-time register, his arm encasing my neck with the gun (less the ammo, a point upon which I insisted, as you can never be too careful) aimed at my temple. He'd drag me out of the shop with the bags and money and then the following week we'd repeat the whole scenario. See the old bird was suffering from Alzheimer's. It worked a treat till a kindly neighbour, a techno-hick, put in video surveillance.

Initially living with Dog was fun but it soon became a real bore. On a nightly basis he'd expound his theories on the social submission of the masses. The slow poisoning of society.

'Cloning,' he'd say, 'it's just a scientific reflection of what's happening to the proletariat.'

'Deep Dog,' and I began to call him my tin man for the more I listened, the more hollow he became.

He attached a meaning to everything.

'Every breath tells me something.'

'It says you're alive Dog.'

'Yeah, I am an organic, living, being. I am the son of the Sun and a daughter of the Earth.'

'You're stoned Dog.'

'What would you know, you're just like them, sent by them to thwart me. To try and break me down. You can't tell me shit.'

Did I mention he was also a certified paranoiac?

Proud of the certificate too. Well let's face it, it was the only piece of official paper he'd ever been, or was likely to be, awarded. He'd had it framed and hung it over the bed.

'They'll get you in the end,' I sneered, smiled sweetly, baring my teeth, doing my utmost to freak him totally.

He began to distrust me after that, sure I had him demented and he'd hide all night under the bed while I slept on top of him.

He knew his place my Dog did.

The best thing about Dog?

The best thing about Dog was I could always blame my farts on him.

Dear Mum,

Dog days but at last my leg has mended and I can walk away. Everything went a bit hazy for a while, summer can do that to you, those stretched-out evenings, hours spent mesmerized, just watching the heat rise. The white rabbit eludes me and I appear to have shrunk to a tiny blot in a huge expansive landscape. I have never seen such vastness, where distance becomes irrelevant and time of no importance and I've slowed right down, no more manic rushing. Going from one extreme to another, cutting out the slow damp decay of past times like a ripe verruca. Do you recall that afternoon when . . . see already I have forgotten.

You'd hate it here Mum, this country I mean. It's so different, vital, young, and vibrant. You'd lag behind, unable to keep up with the pace, ideas, the people. Sometimes I hear your voice, 'what in God's name . . .', that moralizing high tone. Here exists all sorts Mother, shocking mutations, and perversions of what it is to be human. Okay maybe it's me who is mouthing those words, but the further I go the harder it seems to turn back. Season changes are exactly that, not some variation on a winter theme, like at home. Anyhow another one beckons and I feel like re-rooting.

Sorry I missed your birthday, but I did think about you.

Big kiss Mum

Send one back as I could really do with one.

A kiss. What I would have given for a kiss that afternoon outside the Aspidistra. He told me his name was Manfredi Braccia and I kept repeating it, all the way back to Dora's, as if by doing so I would somehow summon him to me.

She said her name was Murrey. Murrey Pogue.

'Where did you get a name like that from?'

'My parents.'

North Clark St, Saturday afternoon, two people talked on the sidewalk till a bus came trundling by. She stuck out an arm, flagged it down and left him staring after her.

The following hours his alone and Manfredi opted to kill a few at the studio and set to, hoisting her image up on his shoulders to carry it there. She'd made him laugh, blurting out the obvious. Was he for real? Her eyebrows arched and eyes flashed, where else would you get a name from? Her voice was softly lyrical, pale, her skin quite pale and eyes watery. Hiding everything behind nothing and almost inconspicuously she slipped into his consciousness. She appeared as a small rebellion in total opposition to the American dream, where everything is displayed in the desire for attention. The national pursuit of perfection and warped out of all recognition, as individuals line up to be sculpted, nipped and tucked, bigger, better, whatever, just so long as they were branded. She seemed to pull the other way, trickling against the tide. He'd noticed her teeth were crooked and nails bitten.

Manfredi climbed the eight floors up to the studio, cursing whomever it was hadn't closed the elevator door, only to find Sol chatting intensely to a Marilyn Monroe lookalike, sitting on the edge of his desk. He hoped he wasn't intruding on potentially important business of the non-commercial kind.

'Manfredi this is Snow White, we're working on a theme for a dwarf conference.'

'If you guys need some privacy,' Manfredi muttered, as if he had interrupted something.

'No need,' came an affected reply from the platinum-haired lady. 'You ready Dodo?' and she jumped from the desk, brushing down her skirt, as a short guy appeared from around the other side.

Sol went to show them out while Manfredi settled down, resting his legs up on the desk, intending to read the paper still clutched beneath his arm.

'Isn't she something else?' Sol yelled, reappearing from the lift shaft, his hands rubbing together in glee. 'And her body language? Was she hot for me or what?'

Manfredi mumbled a response, hoping Sol would leave him in peace.

'What a lady. Hey what do you think?' Sol continued, insistent on gaining attention. 'Queen Vixen,' and he howled.

Manfredi was forced to relent, conversation expected, could not be avoided.

'So Fredi what brings you here? Let me guess, Kelly's realized her major error and dumped you. Am I right?'

She said, 'Maybe some other time, no really I'd like that, it's just, well I've got an audition I have to go to. You know how it is and I can't be late.'

Close up, looking down at her on the sidewalk with her satchel strapped across her chest and face turned upward into his. Manfredi stood tall in indigo jeans and a dark tan leather jacket with his hands thrust deep into his pockets.

Casually he explained himself and thought it odd that she had asked about the girl in Al's, 'Debra? No she's a friend,' then suggested a coffee . . . but she had to go.

'Maybe some other time,' and she touched him lightly on his forearm.

Up close, so clearly defined, she appeared even smaller, which meant he had to lean in further to catch her words before they scattered unheard in the wind. 'Damn I'm going to be late, this always happens, damn.'

Introducing herself, hands met half way and shook, sparking him. Manfredi wanted to know more, to unravel her.

He asked if he could call her.

'Sure,' she said, 'I'd like that, being new to the city and all.'

He had run out of cards, left them in his other coat. Damn but she said,

'You never know maybe I'll bump into you in Al's.'

The bus door swung open. She waved from the

window, looking back at him till the bus turned
sharply out of view.

Sol raised a brow and leant forward,
'Murrey Pogue?' Sol could barely contain his envy.
Escapade after escapade and it wasn't like the guy had
a ten-inch dick, of which Sol was certain, having on
several occasions snuck glances, on purpose.
  'Tell me what kind of fuckwit name is that?'
Manfredi considered a moment.
'Slightly unusual.'
'Believe me it doesn't sound right, she's made it up.'
  Rushing to an audition, that's what she said and
Manfredi assumed she was an actress.
  'Maybe she plays in some daytime soap.'
  Sol's mouth curled upward at the edge and with
snide precision he sneered,
  'Yeah and maybe she's a waitress.'
  'Anyway,' he persevered, 'What about Kelly? I
thought you were meant to be in love with Kelly.'
  'What about Kelly?' Manfredi answered drily,
fiddling with a large steel letter-opener, left lying on the
edge of Sol's desk.
  'Jocelyne gave it to me,' remarked Sol, pulling the
edges of his jacket forward, in an effort to close the gap
but failing due to his bulbous stomach. 'It's an attempt
to keep her presence always in mind. Hey check out
this site.'
  Sol turned his computer round toward Manfredi,
picked up the receiver and hit speed dial.
  'Speaking of which. Hello Joce? . . . Oh it's you
Dinah.' Sounding deflated Sol silently mouthed the
words 'her sister' to Manfredi. 'Is Jocelyne there?'
  Sol cleared his throat,

'Hey, so what we up to this evening?' but his smile swiftly contracted and he spun around, his voice lowering.

'You misunderstood. I said if anything else came up I'd cancel . . . Yeah so nothing came up . . . Okay you're going out . . . Sure it's fine . . . Charlie who? . . . Can't I take an interest in your friends? . . . No it's just you never mentioned him before . . . Charlie's a woman . . . Why didn't you say? . . . Why would I be jealous? . . . Listen have a great time . . . See you whenever . . . Like what? . . . I'm not being like anything . . . I love you okay? I'm gonna marry you. Okay? Later.'

Sol replaced the receiver. He'd begun to sweat lightly and took a handkerchief from his breast pocket wiping it first across his forehead and then beneath his chin.

'So what d'you think?' Sol asked, referring to the dwarf porno page.

'Sol, anyone ever said what a sad person you are?'

Sol thought for a moment. 'My mother, Jocelyne . . . oh yeah, and Nana Finkel. By the way, you doing anything tonight?'

Manfredi had arranged to met Kelly later but was persuaded into having a quick drink.

'Love,' Sol swore, motioning Manfredi to rise and move towards the door, 'women. You got to be careful, even the so-called kosher ones are crazy.'

Then, locking up the studio he turned his attention back to Manfredi. 'Listen you think Jocelyne was winding me up? You think she could be having an affair?'

'Sol the woman adores you. There's no way she'd cheat.'

'But who the fuck would name a girl Charlie? What kind of people do such things?'

'People into cheap perfume.'

'You're right. I'm being stupid. You're right.'

Sol continued with his deliberations, 'You think I should call again?'

Manfredi advised him to wait at least half an hour.

Outside they considered their destination, the sole criteria being proximity and they walked a couple of blocks to the local bar. Dino's was a dismal place with a few men scattered randomly and a single female alco sat hunched over on a stool at the bar counter. Up high in a corner perched a TV with the sound turned down low. The barman wore a look of genuine disinterest and in mid-yawn called out, 'What can I get you boys?'

A pool table beckoned in the far corner and they wandered over, beers in hand. Sol munched through a packet of salted peanuts, aiming in the general direction of his mouth, with a two-in-one chance of striking lucky. Imbibing the spirit of the place, they blue-chalked the ends of their cues, ready to play the best of three. They were lousy and glad no one was round to watch.

An hour later, one game all, Manfredi had sunk his last spot and was lining up the eight ball when the woman sat up at the bar decided to slouch over.

She grinned inanely and raised her empty glass, 'You wanna buy me a drink fellas?'

Licking his index finger and fanning it in her face, Sol was categorical in his refusal.

'Assholes,' she slurred, wiping the word across the table, then hunching over to take the black ball and pocket it.

'Fuck sakes,' hissed Sol, slapping his forehead. 'I could've won.'

'What you say mister?' she squealed, showing a hint

of aggression, drawing attention to the corner.

The barman shouted over, 'Dora, leave the guys alone.'

'I only wanted a fucking drink,' she snarled and turned back.

'Did you see that, did you see that . . .' Sol was getting worked up, Manfredi urged him to leave it and suggested they go elsewhere.

DORA arrived back with a black eye. She'd been in a fight with Dino. He'd had to slug her one after her hassling his clientele. Politely I indicated it would be more helpful if he refused to serve her. Dino told me to mind my own business, offering me up his fist to drive the point home. It's always the same, at the end of a shit awful week he knows that in Dora he has a punchbag at the ready. She gets drunk, hassles guys for money and when Dino thinks she's driven away one too many, he takes her outside. Then, after he's finished, he kicks her back up the stairs to me.

There I was, trying to watch the early Saturday transmission of *Beat the Clock*. It was my favourite programme and every week I'd call in after the show and apply to be on it.

Dora came stumbling in. She crawled over to me, screeching like a wounded pig, stopping right in front of the TV, demanding I clean her up. I hate it when people purposely stand in the way of the screen, blocking it.

I told her to move but she kept weeping, dribbling nonsense on me. I went to get a damp cloth as her nose was bleeding, besides she was wearing one of my jumpers.

That was another thing I hated, the way she helped herself to my stuff without asking, as if they were hers for the taking. When I came back to the settee, I discovered she had plonked herself down right where I'd been sitting and switched channels.

'For chrissakes Dora, I was watching *Beat the Clock*.'

She didn't say anything.

'Dora, it's the only thing I watch.'

She began to mimic me in a high-pitch whine,

'For chrissakes Dora I was . . .'

I felt like whacking her one myself, but she beat me to it and took out her penknife. Dora was big into self-mutilation. Heck if everyone else was having a go at her, then why shouldn't she. One of her favourite inflictions was cutting in deep beneath her fingernails. She had the most beautiful long nails, a good couple of inches, painstakingly painted in patterns and it flummoxed me why she bothered when she let the rest of herself get in such a mess. She once claimed to have shredded a guy's back, clawing away at his skin till he begged for mercy. A sad victory, owing to the circumstance of her being thirteen at the time and him taking advantage.

I took the penknife out of her hand and threw her a towel. There was nothing else for it but to give her a hug and tell her she was loved. I sat down on the arm of the chair and began stroking her hair.

'Dora it's okay, really it's okay.'

It really wasn't okay, she'd lost control of everything, her very self disintegrating and I wiped the trickle of blood from under her nostril while she began reminiscing about way back then, when things seemed a lot better. When we had fun and life wasn't such a struggle.

'You and me Murrey, we go back a long way. We're two of a kind.'

I'd have begged to differ but it didn't seem the right occasion.

'Sure, we're mates.'

'Soul mates Murrey.' She began to sob quietly. 'Tell me I'm beautiful.'

'Dora first time I saw you, I thought, who is that woman, she must be a supermodel.'

'Did ya Murrey? Did ya?'

I met Dora on my travels, we became entangled through a third party. It had nothing to do with choice.

We fell together.

It was following the period when I'd plunged into a black hole, Dog stench kisses on my breath with an attitude to match.

Beneath a bus-stop at the corner of a street.

'Hey you waiting for anyone Doll?'

He took me by surprise.

'A miracle,' I answered.

'Jump in girl, you just found one.'

Patting the red plastic of the seat, he tilted his head, so his eyes peeped out over his shades, 'Where you at girl?'

'I'm at here,' I replied, pulling the door closed.

He scratched his head, 'You ain't making no sense.'

'Phew.' See I thought it was just me.

He drove me in his convertible to the shoreline and we ran down on to the beach and into the sea. We danced amongst the waves, within the belly of the ocean and he kissed me so hard I thought I was drowning.

'I'm so happy I found you,' I cried. 'A miracle.'

My body shaking and it felt like my skin was about to give in, about to tear open when he said.

'Naw I was just kidding, I'm an atheist. My name's Zebedi.'

Zebedi was like that, liked to play games but would always end up cheating.

He was always cheating on me.

Somewhere along the road I must have taken a wrong turn. I had been wandering a while far from home, no turning back, actually there wasn't a turning in sight. Zebedi was the first person to cross my path in a long time. I knew he wasn't the one but he did so dazzle me. He wore a dark suit with his chest bare beneath, trainers on his feet, rings on his fingers, bedecked in gold, black hair, green eyes and a goatee beard.

He whispered softly, 'You gal, why you just like a sparkly jewel that needs a good polishing, worth a fortune to me.'

I took it to mean I was priceless, deluding myself but I had to believe in something.

And I'd wake him in the middle of the night and shake him by his shoulders.

'You are the one, you have to be.'

'Go back to sleep,' he'd murmur, rolling up and away from me.

Zebedi never once asked where I came from, he was of the opinion a woman should retain a hint of mystery about her.

This suited me fine and in the beginning, he did so make me glow. He brought me places I never knew existed. For with a flick of his wrist he would sprinkle stardust on me. Flying high, like I was floating on clouds. So much stardust, too much and it got so the

73

days submerged into one long blazing night. Zebedi claimed he had the power, the powder, to halt my ageing process. I stepped into a capsule, encapsulating time and for a while thought I was doing myself some good.

Zebedi was real popular. He hung on the borders of the entertainment industry and knew all sorts of people, A list, B list, C list. We'd access to the best parties but never hung round too long.

Zipping here and there, like a happy alchemist, his pockets full of powders, pills and potions. A modern day wishmaker for your every desire could be catered for.

He had a condo, close to the sea, his place a constant buzz. Like one big happy family except the faces changed daily. Always laughing and in a good mood, he was infectious. No, truly, and I'd call Zebedi my Virus, pissed at him for spreading himself about.

'But Doll, you know it's you I love. You think any of the other broads would bring me breakfast in bed? I mean those hoes, you think they'd know what a pressed shirt was?'

I figured at least he was being totally honest. I mean he was really up front and never made me feel left out, matter of fact, he asked me to join in loads. Of course I'd throw my eyes to the heavens so I wouldn't have to see what was happening.

When I tried to talk to him about things, you know, personal stuff, Zeb said he didn't care. He told me nothing really mattered and I should live for the moment. I envied his nonchalance for ages, until I realized, he really didn't care, he'd even forgotten my name.

He'd taken to calling me bitch. Bitch, I kinda liked it,

made me seem hard, toughened. I was hardening up.

So blind and then one day Zebedi sat me down, he took both my hands in his and said,

'You're not a real player. This has to stop.'

'I am, I am,' I implored, 'I can play as well as anyone.'

I just wanted to belong.

'You sure? You one hundred percent sure, you're up to it?'

I nodded fervently.

'Okay,' he answered and he put me on the game.

Dear Mom,

I'm working flat out. This is a blue-sky city, a place of constant summer, on the surface everything looks pretty clean and I'm cleaning up. I've hitched with a guy called Zebedi who looks out for and after me. I'm not sure you'd approve of him, I'm not sure I do but I'm having a nice time, or time passes pleasantly enough. I'm hoping something better may come along and I'm sure it will, cause I'm meeting loads of people.

Funny old life isn't it? I hope you're laughing.

Kisses and hugs . . .

Then the complaints started.

'I knew you weren't up to it,' Zebedi snorted.

Clients began to report on me, said I was too pushy. Too much in their face.

'Well there's no pleasing everyone,' I answered back.

'Look there are unwritten rules, things you don't do.'

'I was just being friendly.'

'Kissing is not on, kissing is not required. Do you understand?'

'No Zebedi, I don't understand.'

'I'm taking you off my books.'

It was then I realized, I'd fallen off the Magic Roundabout.

Dora was one of the original members of Zebedi's 'clan'. She'd been hanging out with him since the age of fourteen. He said he'd make her a star and put her in the skin flicks. A fallen star, for before she knew it she was a high-class escort girl, and as the years began to take their toll, her status dropped and habit worsened. I'd look at Dora as a warning.

Dora told me Zebedi had booted her out, claiming it was for her own good. 'There'll be no more nothing for you bitch,' his parting words, till she got cleaned up. Instead she'd come to Chicago hoping to trace her natural mother, who'd had her fostered at the age of two and hadn't seen her since.

Just before Dora passed out, she'd started on about going back to Zebedi. How he'd look after her, treat her like a lady. I didn't want to take her hope away. 'Sure Dora, everything will be fine, you'll find Zebedi and it will all work out.' Patting her back with soothing words in tandem with her snoring and then I put her to bed.

Staring down at her, I had no pity or compassion to spare. Her hospitality served only to highlight all I wanted to escape. I prayed that if there was a God he'd take her. Then I ran down to the local Kmart and got myself half a litre of ice cream to chill my insides.

When I arrived back, Dora had gone. There was a note pinned to the door, saying she'd left to try and find Zebedi, that I could stay put, as long as I paid the rent and by the way, there were three months owing.

Clicking on the radio to full volume, I waited for a good song, something to aptly capture my mood and as I waited the sweet cream soothed my insides. Then hearing the right note struck I jumped up, flicked open an old Zippo and waved my hands above my head.

IT was Sunday, a week further into winter and Manfredi sensed a hovering cold due to a sudden drop in temperature.

Sat opposite Debra, his gaze unfocused, flitted from one side of the room to another, then back to the table were he played with a beer mat, shredding it into tiny pieces. They'd come to brunch and listen to some jazz at the Soul Kitchen. Tomas, Debra's boyfriend who played sax was with his band, the Zeitgeist Zephyrs, setting up in the corner.

'Face it Manfredi she hasn't called by Al's once this week.'

Manfredi had hoped Debra would throw some feminine logic on the situation, but all she had done was spread doubt, as if every question should have a reasonable answer.

'You think she deliberately fobbed me off?'

'Manfredi it's possible, plausible, who knows.'

'No way, I'm too discerning.'

'Look, first thing she does is jump on a bus, makes some excuse about auditions or whatever. Switch sides, if unknown to you, a woman butts in on your day, yakety-yak, "I've seen you before let's get it together", what would you think?'

'Weirdo,' she answered for him, slamming the word down on the table, 'is exactly what you'd think.'

Put so bluntly Manfredi conceded Debra had a point, but wasn't convinced.

'What about intuition, like when you just know. Don't you ever get like that?'

Debra looked at him blankly. 'That kind of shit is movie domain.'

'You're just bitter and twisted,' sneered Manfredi.

'Anyhow what's going on with Kelly?'

'Ah Kelly . . .' Manfredi's eyes ceased dancing. Things were going smoothly, to plan and maybe that was it, their affair seemed almost contrived. She'd bought him an electric toothbrush and cleared a drawer so he could leave some of his stuff at hers. 'Look Kelly is really great it's just . . .'

'Manfredi you always do this, minute you get someone, you lose interest.'

'That's not fair.'

'Sure or you stay with her until someone else comes along. You're so shallow, it's the pursuit of the unattainable for you.'

'I just have a low boredom threshold.'

'Bullshit you're scared.'

Manfredi considered whether he really was so transparent in his choices. For the past few years he'd maintained a steady system of pursuit and abandonment. Due in the main to his great heartburn on his arrival in Chicago, when his trusting abilities had been singed to the point of indentation. Whitewashed in deceit he didn't like to dwell on it. Besides that was then, in the past, neatly stacked away and time had licked the scar.

'How about you?' he asked turning his attention to Debra.

Debra had been seeing Tomas on and off for about

a year. On and off being the operative word, as he was happily married with three kids. Tomas had emerged from a street brawl outside of Al's. He stumbled in for sympathy and to sound off in safety about neighbourhood scum. Debra quietened him down, listening as a stream of Hungarian curses spewed forth, thinking he had the most wonderful accent. Initially she had fallen in love with his voice. Tomas was easy, partially available and physically they suited one another, but the fact he was so comfortable with the situation had started to irritate Debra and that there was no one else on her horizon, was worse.

'So what you going to do?'

Debra sighed, 'I don't know, I mean you get to a stage and you know the story, you know the limits, so little surprises me anymore.' She looked him directly in the eyes. 'You sure you're not shielding some Mr Wonderful from me?'

'Debra you know all my friends.'

'What about a last resort?'

'A drink do?'

She smiled across at him then lit a cigarette. 'Look, Tomas makes me laugh and fills a gap. What more could a girl ask for?'

'Plenty.'

'Idealist.'

'Fatalist.'

'Jerk.'

Manfredi shrugged his shoulders and gave in. Debra had to have the last line, a skill picked up from waitressing, where the put-down was usually better than the food.

'So what are you going to say to Kelly?'

'Nothing.' He watched Debra's expression change to

a glowering scowl, thinking bastard. 'No really, she's leaving, I don't have to do anything.'

In bed, the night before, Kelly had mentioned she'd been offered a transfer to a New York branch of the office. She'd applied for the position a while back. Her decision expected on Monday.

Debra pulled deeply on her cigarette.

'So Kelly slips out of the frame and you move in on Murrey, kind of thing.'

Manfredi hadn't thought of it in such mercenary terms. It wasn't really as clear cut as that, as if he'd planned it.

'Hey, I don't even know if I'll see Murrey again and look it's a really good opportunity for Kelly. I mean who am I to hold her back?'

'In other words, a case of I'm not into long-distance relationships. Let's see what happens when you return?'

He shrugged his shoulders, 'I'll just go get those drinks.'

Heading for the bar Manfredi caught sight of Sol standing by the door of the Ladies, a surreptitious cigarette in his hand, the smoke billowing out uninhaled. Caught in the act, Sol felt the need to explain,

'Had to, five minute respite from the big J. Over there. She's got friends staying from Washington. Married friends. And you?'

Across the room and Manfredi pointed to Debra.

Raising his eyebrows Sol looked back unimpressed, 'That's Murrey! I mean Manfredi, weren't you exaggerating a little?'

'Jesus Sol. That's Debra, a friend,' and Sol, easily undercut, stubbed out his cigarette, his minor insult deflating to quickly change the subject.

'Yeah well. They're going through the honeymoon photos, I think Jocelyne's trying to ladle it on. Like Miami isn't good enough!'

'She's cute though,' continued Sol indicating Debra.

'Sol you're getting married in a couple of months.'

'What does she do?'

'Manageress of Al's.'

'Ach too bad.' Sol sighed like Debra had blown her chances. Jocelyne was an orthodontist, professional status being a requirement of Sol Marksman's relationship qualifications. Manfredi ordered the drinks while Sol went to brush his teeth in the Men's. Walking back to the table Manfredi introduced them. Sol offered Debra one of his ingratiating grins.

'Check the band out, never heard anything like it.'

'Yeah you like them?' asked Debra turning round to face him.

'Like them? They stink, nearly put me off my food. Enjoy the rest of your meal.' And with that he left them to wander back over to a gleaming set of pincers.

'What in God's name was that?' asked Debra.

Manfredi finding it hard to curtail a smile said,

'That Debra is exactly what you were referring to.'

'What?'

'A last resort.'

IT was getting cold, touching sub-zero. My floral services fast becoming obsolete. Joe from the Weiner Circle had gone to Texas to see his sister competing in some all-weather rodeo competition and I ended up spending the whole week selling dogs. For a split second I imagined I'd been draped in a celestial silver lining but it didn't turn out so good, more like a cloudburst.

It began with the annual arrival of a pesky health inspector. One of the Weiner Circle, and there's always one, had been selling the real McCoy, hot dog (well you get what you pay for), and on this occasion it happened to be Joe. There was uproar, front-page news and a troop of vegetarians came marching victorious through the park, eager to flex their peace-loving muscles. Of course it all got out of hand, culminating with them trashing the stand. Joe arrived back furious, he hadn't been covered for what was termed terrorist activity, thought it justifiable to blame me, then decided to sue me for damage of his stand. This left me in a very precarious position. In terms of status, I was a visitor who'd overstayed her welcome, barely visible. I lay low for a few days and kept myself busy by calling into radio shows. It can get kinda lonely holed up on your own and I had to talk to someone. Anyhow I didn't get a chance to call by Al's.

By this stage I was in dire need of a job. The last interview had been for a sales assistant in one of those fashionable boutiques and had begun on a pretty good note.

The owner asked me which designer I was au fait with.

I answered, 'They're all okay by me.'

He peered down his nose at me, flaring his nostrils so I could admire his perfectly manicured recesses. Not a nasal hair in sight.

'What colour,' he demanded, 'was last season's black?'

This I assumed was a trick question and guessed grey, he told me I was right.

Next he inquired if I could gaze down at patrons and make people feel like shite the moment they walked through the door, especially if they looked slightly shoddy or had small children tugging out of them.

I looked at this guy and he said I was making him uncomfortable. Kept eyeballing him and he said he was getting bad vibes off me. I was staring him straight in the face and he said he wouldn't trust me as far as he could throw me. My eyes focused in on him and he told me to get out of his shop, immediately.

People never cease to amaze me.

Approaching the end of my tether, I figured it was a case of keeping the faith, my morning mantra and everything would work out fine. I just had to pace myself. Though on recollection the last time things were this bad, they then got worse, another little lesson learnt on my travels.

I left Zebedi without saying goodbye. Perhaps it was rude of me, especially considering his hospitality but in the circumstances I didn't know what else to do.

Basically I took off with everything I could lay my hands on. Totting up those wages he said he'd been keeping for me, in a high-interest safety account. So safe there was ne'er a trace of it.

Claiming otherwise, Zebedi had the capacity to be incredibly possessive and first chance I got, I grabbed a ride and sped out of there, aiming for the back of beyond. Reached my goal in good time and found myself dumped on some godforsaken highway. At least I was safe in the knowledge Zebedi wouldn't come looking for me here, being a tad out of his range.

I had landed in the middle distance, as the road stretched out before me devoid of life and lay behind me, empty as an echo. Due in short to another lingual misunderstanding.

I swear, these people speak another language. When the driver said I could pay him in kind, I told him he was a sweet bloke, even though he was grotesquely overweight, with an overpowering body odour. I remarked on his generosity of spirit, his warm welcome, loving touch, wandering hands, no I didn't want to suck his dickstick even though I'm sure it was succulent. I applauded his realistic threatening manner, please let go of me, I shrieked, such bravado on his part and he said I was giving him the come on, by being evasive. He was most aggressive so I played soap. Slipped through his fingers and jumped.

Glad I'd managed to get this far, I fell down on my knees to pray. While I was there I asked for some respite, a little bit of nurturing love.

Lord, I said, it wouldn't go amiss.

Within minutes the Mulrooneys appeared.

They picked me up on a disused interstate section, my thumb extended in hopeful conviction. The car snail-pacing the borders, obviously on the lookout and they eased up beside me and lowered down the window.

It was a warm day, Mr Mulrooney was sweating, wiping a kerchief over the bald pate of his head which he stuck out the window and drawled in undertones,

'Excuse me ma'am but have you been saved?'

'In the nick of time by the looks of things.'

They asked were I was headed. I answered I was submitting to the will of our Lord,

'God alone knows.'

They approved my logic, told me to climb in the back.

I was accepted as a kinder spirit, quite literally as

it happened, but heck I felt like a pilgrim and any home is a good one, as long as it has a roof, or so I thought.

Maureen and Bill Mulrooney lived in the small town of Hogwash off the mainstream interstate.

They put me in the room that had belonged to their daughter who, at the tender age of sixteen, had disappeared without a trace. Last seen running wildly down the highway thus providing the impetus for the Mulrooneys daily drives up and down it, as a form of penance.

Her room was sweet, candy coloured, adolescent scented, fluffy furry toys lined up along the pillow, a yellow floral nightie folded neatly on the bed. Hair grips and ribbons, pictures of church youth meetings and horses' heads with lines of insipid piety or platitude pasted all over the place. On the small study table lay unfinished homework, a math equation uncompleted, her school clothes name-tagged.

Everything 'just so', like she had popped out and was expected back any minute.

Bill and Maureen threw out all my stuff and I found myself in Emmy-Lou's shoes. I gave thanks for small mercies as we happened to be the same size.

God-fearing simple folk, they fed me on cherry pie and homemade lemonade, went to extremes to make me comfortable both physically and spiritually. They regarded me as a God-given daughter, so I asked them for pocket money. Make yourself at home, they said, so I took out my address book and spent hours on the phone. They demanded I go to chapel with them and I threw a fit, the minister rushed round and baptized me on the spot.

*

Podding peas in the kitchen one afternoon, I pondered aloud on the fate of their daughter.

'Maureen?'

'Child how many times do I have to tell you. Call me momma.'

'What was Emmy-Lou running away from?'

Unprovoked, this wholesome American mother let a plate, unfortunately one that had been handed down through the generations since the Founding Fathers, crash smash to the floor.

Oops-a-daisy.

'Emmy-Lou,' she high-pitched hollered, well, screeched, 'You did not run away you were devilled away.'

'Oh right,' I said, wondering why I had bothered to come back.

Later that evening, cringing as we flicked through the family album, a daily exercise to conjure forth my lapsed memory, Maureen was indoctrinating me, about the time Minister Thomson had held me up as a shinning example in chapel, for doing some good deed or other.

'Do you remember Emmy, you were such a good child?'

'Look,' I replied exasperated, 'How many times do I have to tell you, I'm not Emmy-Lou.'

This didn't go down well, snapping the album shut Maureen marched over to the kitchen door where a leather belt hung, unleashed it from its hook, then marched onward Christian soldier to the sink, taking in her hand the large bar of cracked yellow Sunshine soap.

'Now which is it to be child? Which is it to be?'

I thought her reaction most extreme and opted for the latter.

*

Somehow I knew it was going to be a struggle to extricate myself from the Mulrooney household.

One afternoon, whilst out driving, I casually let slip my intentions,

'I better be making a move soon.'

We swerved into a lay-by, they bound my hands and feet and put me in the boot of the car. Told me there'd be all hell to pay if I stepped out of line, so I decided to hop it, but a fellow brethren spotted me on the road and brought me back.

Maureen and Bill were waiting on the porch,

'Do you have anything to say for yourself young lady?'

'I . . .' didn't get a word in and anyhow they couldn't hear my screams locked up in the attic. It was there I realized I was going to have to change strategy. I accepted my lot, graciously turning the other cheek to plot wildly, bide my time and do the utmost to earn their trust, which would allow me ('Aw please Momma, please, I'll never ever ever be bad again . . . Pops you're the best-ist in the whole wide world') a place on the Jesus Loves You Youth Convention in Portland Oregon.

Christ but it was hard going. The Convention was held on the outer regions of the city in a disused hospice, there but for the grace of God, and we sang and we clapped, freaking out on our Lord's vibes and I signed up for the Best Trance Convert Contest, the prize being you got to go into town and spread the word.

Breakdancing saved my life, though personally speaking, I thought the spastic was better. Anyhow, adorned with my crown of thorns, off I went with the Legion of Mercy Angels in their minibus, to convert the lost and hell-damned.

What better place to find wandering souls than a rail station, my suggestion, and when the first train began its pull out of the station, I went with.

Hallelujah, but it was a relief to be on the road again. The good life had led me astray and holed up in some desolate place I drank to my plight and drank to a future and drank till I found a way out.

Mother,

Fuck it and I know I shouldn't, but I do. Excuse my squiggly writing but I am in a bar and seeing double, I am seeing double because you are always there. Oh maudlin mother me, whenever I do anything slightly amiss you are there. Can you not at least stay three paces back woman? Like in the good old days when you pushed me round. Oh sorry. I'm sorry, sorry before I even start. You know I really love you, see I am crying now, a tear has smudged one of the sorrys. It will probably please you to know that at last, I understand exactly what I am seeking. I am at present love-seek.

Tell me Ma when did the breast become a fist?

Yours,

Murrey

PS. I only say this to you because I can.

I suckled long and hard on that notion, when nurturing alters to become a slow poisoning of fears. Too long, for the sweetness curdled and bitter I could not stomach it and spat it back in the face of my mother.

Well, who else was there to blame?

Eager to shrug off my inheritance, I had ambled

disheartened, back to Dora's flat.

Another joyless day and desperate to pull this skin from off of me, to get to the heart of the matter, I stood naked in front of the wardrobe mirror. The reflection not quite fitting, a diluted version of my mother and dressed in her genes, it unnerved me how I did not seem to fit myself. Motionless in front of the telling glass, watching this image fade to transparency. Sometimes I guess you have to die a little, you cease to exist in any capacity other than merely functioning, then your mind relaxes and unburdened life becomes easier.

Maybe it was the dying part I wasn't quite getting right. My father used to say, if you do something you should do it properly. He always did things properly. Abandoning the pair of us without a by your leave.

Fuck it, if I was going to take that route then I wanted to make a statement. I wanted it to be serene and beautiful. I set myself a deadline. Gave myself twenty-four hours to turn my whole life round or else it was time to call it a day.

Then and wouldn't you only warrant it, a free local paper was pushed through the door. Working my way down the columns, I began to scan the classified section and noticed the following ad:

You too could be earning XYZ a week. Three whole letters with the potential to acquire the rest of the alphabet. (Plus commission.) Interested? Pick up the phone and dial Clear Glazers on the following number.

Sat by the window I looked up: Clear Glazers was right across the street. Rubbing my eyes in disbelief, I could just about make out the director from the window. Dressed in a cheap suit, he was giving it some aural, resting his sharp tongue upon a lady friend's earpiece. I dialled, the director picked up the receiver.

'I'm calling about the job,' I said.

He paused then asked, 'When can you start?'

'Right away.'

'Lady I like your pro-active attitude, see you in five.'

Guess I knew things were going to have to get better. I painted on some lippy, knowing I'd have to keep my wits about me, and ran across the street.

MANFREDI'S head was pounding, nose streaming and housebound all week, he'd been jacking up on vitamin C. He hadn't seen Murrey since outside the Aspidistra, no coincidental run-ins and he felt slightly mocked by the lead in, when you believe something is going somewhere, like a sneeze holding back, about to explode, then dispersing with zero relief.

He hated that.

A love teaser, the tension of expectation dwindling as the days rolled by. This, compounded by a niggling feeling of self-pity, as Manfredi had found himself on his own again.

The date of Kelly's transfer had wavered between postponement and being brought forward. The latter prevailed and all of a sudden she left. Before her departure the predestined homily on the failure of long-distance relationships teetered on the edge of Manfredi's tongue but Kelly surprised him and took the words from out of his mouth. Pre-empting him, Kelly asserted that in her opinion, and with how things were, it would be better if they called a halt to the proceedings. She actually said, maybe we could call a halt to the proceedings and wait till I return.

'Why?' he asked, 'When things are going so well?'

She reckoned it would be better, for both of them. There wouldn't have to be any misunderstandings, misdemeanours, mistakes or ties to become entangled in. He agreed but not without sufficient protestation.

Either way, he was put on hold, holding out in his apartment, till the fuzz surrounding his head lifted and the sneeze ignited. Shuffling about aimlessly, from one room to the next, the only human contact available was captured in a mechanical box. Daily gravitations toward the TV set where he would grind to a halt and hover there static, as time inched forward. Boredom always brought with it a despondent listlessness. Unable to bear another episode of *Chicago Hope*, Manfredi was determined to do something useful. Sat in the tatty armchair, he cast his eye over the room and decided a rearrangement was in order. This, a reoccurring thought, entailed spending the next three hours shifting his furniture from one side of the room to the other.

It would begin with Manfredi moving the his ex's paintings from off the walls to the cupboard, designated to contain all that stuff you hadn't the heart to chuck but hoped one day to either recycle or sell. Then, when the room reached a certain chaotic pitch, the two glaring wall patches would force him to reconsider. Doing his utmost to convince himself he would paint the apartment first chance he got, he always failed dismally, ending the evening by returning everything to its original position. Finally flopping back down into his worn leather chair, Manfredi drowsed off into a frustrated realm.

He woke in a cramped and painful position and checking the time on the stereo the wretched hour of 4.30 a.m. blinked back. Trying to retain that half state of slumber, Manfredi plodded into the bathroom to pee, then to his room, peeled off his clothes and crawled beneath the covers. In the darkness his arm extended outward to reach for a glass of water, left on his radio alarm on the beside table, when a sneeze crept up on him, exploding with a shudder that his whole body responded to. He had knocked over the glass, tipping it over the edge, to clatter on the wooden floor, clumsily missing the soft landing of his pile of discarded clothes. This accompanied by the radio blaring into action, his finger on the button.

Manfredi groaned aloud, reaching out once more, to turn the damn thing off, but was arrested by the drone of the insomniac DJ and then her voice. Murrey on air and he wondered whether it was really happening, looking at the clock, 4.45 a.m.

'Where did you get a name like that?' asked the amused DJ.

'From my parents,' came her reply.

'And what has you up at this time?'

'I was dreaming.'

'Don't you have to be asleep to dream?'

'It woke me up.'

'Was it a sexy dream?'

'Not really. It was about this woman born with too few layers of skin.'

'Freaky.'

'She goes to the end of the world in search of love.'

'And does she find it?'

'Yeah but . . .'

'Well that sounds real horny. So folks here's Murrey

Pogue singing the all-time Louis Armstrong favourite.'

Manfredi could hardly believe it. He heard her cough to clear her throat, then launch into 'We have all the time in the world', attempting to mimic the low soft growl of the master, forcing her chords down, as far as they would go and failing abysmally.

She clapped herself at the end, the DJ was cracking up.

'So Murrey tell us a little more about yourself.'

'I guess just like everyone else, I'm looking for love.'

'You don't have a man in your life?'

'Not at the moment.'

'And what exactly are you after?'

'A strong protective arm, a certain smell, soft skin, large heart, two arms, two legs, a head and torso, an ability to laugh, to cry, to share, to give, to take,' she was on a roll.

'You wanna be more specific,' the DJ was humouring her, she paused a moment.

'You still there Murrey?'

'The softest of lips. Red, ruby red, rubescent like a woman's. That's exactly what I want.'

'Well, we wish you all the best and pleasant dreams. Folks that was Murrey Pogue singing, "All the time in the world", if you want to vote her as best singer just call us here on . . .'

Manfredi couldn't believe it, he'd tuned into her, like they were on the same wavelength.

He tried memorizing the number of the station, determined to ring it in the morning, repeating it over and over till he fell asleep.

Manfredi woke late to the shrill sound of his buzzer. Morning had arrived, way too abruptly. He groped his way to the intercom, his vision blurred and head heavy.

'Hey Manfredi.'

Manfredi attempted a greeting but it sounded more like a grunt.

Debra, on the way back from the gym, with only a few moments to spare, had rested her index finger on the bell of apartment number 1147. Her buzzing insistence forced him out from his bed and over to the door.

'What's up?'

'Thought I'd call by, see how you were feeling?'

'Getting there.'

'Listen she called by Al's last night.'

'Huh?'

'The cute girl in Al's.'

'What? Murrey?'

Debra's conversational blitzkrieg tactics had Manfredi playing tag with his thoughts. 'What . . . are you coming up?'

'Can't, I'm on my way to work . . .'

'Wait a sec, I'll come down.'

He threw on some clothes, splashed his face with water. His head splitting and grabbing an aspirin he swallowed it, then rushed out of the apartment. Found the elevator out of order and ran down fourteen flights, cursing as he flew. Debra was waiting for him in the foyer, wrapped in sheepskin and peeking out at him from under a knitted bobble hat.

'Roll on summer,' she sighed.

Manfredi, his heart beating, blood jumping, blurted it out,

'You won't believe this,' and he told Debra about the phone-in chat show.

'Weird, don't you think?'

'You sure you weren't dreaming?'

'Swear to you.'

'Maybe it was someone else.'

'No way, there's no way, I'm telling you Debra it's like it's fated,' and breathless he asked,

'So did you talk to her?'

Debra described how Murrey had dropped by the previous day for a coffee and . . .

'Dee, what did she say?'

'She's new to Chicago, got a job in telesales, works in a place called Clear Glazers.'

'And that's it?'

'Yeah, damn I forgot my magic wand.'

'She leave a number?'

'Uh-uh.'

Manfredi walked Debra out to her car, parked haphazardly, the hazard lights flicking, a counterfeit disabled driver sticker stuck to the window.

'She'll be there from 5 p.m.'

'How do you know?'

'She said she worked the evening shift, starting from five.'

Debra climbed into the car and blew Manfredi a kiss,

'Fancy Manzoni's tomorrow night? Tomas is playing solo.'

'Yeah maybe, yeah sure, I'll give you a call.'

She started up the ignition, a fierce acceleration as if the car should have been a bike. Debra used to have a bike, a Yamaha, a beauty. In her early twenties she'd been big into the freedom of the road, eventually she'd sold it to some New York bulldyke called Jess.

'Call her. She's cute. I mean if I was that way inclined . . .'

Manfredi's spirits lifted and the idea of spending another day confined in his apartment was wholly unappealing. He showered, threw on some clothes and decided to spend some time at the studio.

There he found Sol, his head buried in his hands, making low moans.

'Hey what's up?'

Startled, Sol raised his brow.

'You won't believe this Manfredi.'

Jocelyne had given Sol his walking papers.

'Jocelyne and I are finito-completo,' each syllable, machine gunned out of his mouth, 'No more.'

Manfredi looked over to the small pile of mail on his desk and then back to the small pile of male, unshaven, probably hadn't slept for the past few days and guessed the latter took priority.

'When did it happen?'

Sol sighed heavily, 'Monday, I'll be fine. I'll be fine,' and he gestured half-hearted, palms down as if placating himself, before turning them over to declare, 'I've had enough, I mean if it's like this before the wedding. You making some coffee?'

Manfredi nodded and went to make some.

'Typical and just when I need to get some major dentistry work done. She timed it on purpose Manfredi.'

'It's probably wedding nerves.'

'Don't even go there Man. Listen I'm round at hers Monday night, going through the invites, talking about the catering, you know the usual.'

Jocelyne had been tetchy all day. She was focusing in on Sol's receding hairline and beady eyes. He'd come straight over from work with a list of fifty caterers.

'And Manfredi may I just remind you here, I'm a conference organizer. Like I know how to organize. She, may I point out, deals in teeth . . . I'm telling her, from my experience. My experience . . .'

She worked her way down over him, everything about Sol grated on her nerves. His face, his smile, his decaying molar, his mouth opened, closed, the overall bite and line of his jaw. She hadn't planned to say anything, do anything but they seemed to have been preparing for the wedding for years. She had bought the dress, begun to diet, he was talking non-stop, going through the proposed menus. He was deliberating on whether the napkins should be two-ply or three-ply, or cloth, embroidered or printed with their initials or a picture.

'So *what do you think Joce, like your input would be appreciated?*'

'I told her some input would be appreciated. That's two sugars.'

Manfredi handed Sol a mug.

Jocelyne snapped, something went inside of her and she realized she didn't care anymore, that frankly, she didn't give a damn.

'She's really having a go, nag, nag, nag and I'm the one doing all the work here, you know. So I said "Frankly Joce you disappoint me," and at this stage she was blubbering, pleading but what about the wedding? I don't give a damn I said. You know, there's always a cut-off point, when you say to yourself, enough is enough. I said to her "I don't give a damn."'

'You think you'll get back together?'

Sol had a pained look on his face, his mouth was twitching.

'I've tried ringing, she isn't picking up. Then last night . . .'

Sol switched his phone to speaker and dialled Jocelyne's number, an automated voice replied, 'This number is out of service.'

'What about her work?'

'I've been calling every hour, her assistant says she's gone out of town for a few days.'

'Probably give her some time to cool down.'

'Manfredi wise up. It's a lie. I hired a private dick. She ain't even away.'

Manfredi advised Sol to back off a little.

'You think?' asked Sol, 'Yeah, maybe you're right. Yeah fuck her. It's her loss right?'

Manfredi did his best to sound as reassuring as possible.

They dialled in some sushi, while Sol got working on his address list. Of course he was trying hard not to show how upset he was, calling up every chick he knew in a 350km radius and asking them on dates. By the time Manfredi was ready to leave the studio, Sol had been on the line for a solid three hours and had accrued one date and two potentials. The definite being a wrong number.

'Hey what about that half-sister of yours, what's she like?'

'I don't have a sister.'

'Sure you do, she called about a month ago.'

'Sol I don't have a sister.'

'Don't play the protective brother with me.'

'Sol, I swear on the American constitution. I don't have a sister.'

'What good is that, you're a Canadian.'

Sometimes it was best to walk away.
'Night Sol.'

Manfredi arrived home after seven. Twenty-past, by the time he had climbed fourteen flights upwards. He was panting, the incline was always worse, he cursed the building and back in the apartment he picked up the phone. Clear Glazers and he got the number from directory enquiries. He pushed the buttons, the tone dialling . . . it clicked and he heard an automated voice, 'Hi there, you've reached Clear Glazers, all our operatives are busy right now . . .'

IF only my mother could see me now . . . a strange emotion swept through me, the distant recognition of jubilation. Nothing's ever really that bad, it's just a matter of perspective. See, good fortune had fallen upon me, I had a nice warm place to lay my head, enough food to line my belly. I had a job in telesales and a soft reassuring voice.

We followed a script, our words penned to pitter-patter in the hope of bamboozling some poor sod into buying double glazing. The place was run like an incident room, cases written on a board, leads to be solved, sold to.

All leads had to be classified, clarified and typified, which meant we targeted people who couldn't really afford it, but felt they were missing out. Market research, neat percentages the numerically inclined can relate to, made it easy, such research being the American for 'truth'. You want it, they got it. Or you don't know you want it, but you're going to get it and I guess it's a supply and demand thing.

I could have done a billion things but the telesales office was a cushy number, or so I liked to think. Anyhow I was working alongside an ex-stripper, ex-sales assistant and a former stockbroker which reassured me somewhat. They said they had had to duck out of the rat race, the pressure had been unbearable, their lives lay in ruination.

This was easy money.

At a price.

It was early evening, I was working the late shift, sat beside Dot the former stockbroker.

Dot had shown me the ropes the day before. She had frizzy hair and caramel skin. So beautiful and I wanted to probe her, tongue pink plush, I wanted to lick it but you must never mix business with pleasure, it's an unwritten rule, something I learned the hard way from Zebedi.

She hummed in tune and I advised her to consider singing as a career move, her voice sounded amazing. I mentioned this radio station which held nightly competitions in search of the best voice on air. Thought it only right to warn her the competition was fixed. The night before I'd called in and an operatic windbag had beaten me by some bizarre percentage.

'Like a hundred per cent. Can you believe it? I mean I used to sing in the school choir.'

She asked where I came from.

'Far side of beyond,' I answered.

'And how come you ended up here?' she pried.

'You really want to know?' And she looked at me quizzically. 'Certain?'

'Yeah.'

Okay and I drew in a huge breath.

It was by then too late to turn back.

Outward and onward.

Onward and I set off from my home on a May morning.

I left with an image of my mother snuffling in the kitchen. We had sat down uneasily to share in some moments of blood ties. It felt unfamiliar, uncomfortable and I kept my eye on the clock on the wall and every so often would check my pockets to make sure the ticket was there. She had made drop scones for me and we'd melted butter over them and spread home-made jam upon them. Sweet insipid and leaning toward me, she asked softly, what it was I wanted and softly I answered her.

To never end up like you.

Alone and weak.

And she didn't answer me.

She never said a word.

I pushed the chair beneath the table, quiet as a mouse.

'I'll be on my way so.'

Loitering in the hallway, the familiar smell, hanging off the walls and I took a deep breath of remembrance, my coat from off the banister and a last look upward.

I was waiting for an apology to rise in my throat or for herself to wander through with misted eyes. Before I left, I wanted to return and further. But when you have gone that bit too far, said the unnecessary truth that dug a little too deep, a fear is voiced and it changes everything. The outcome lingering, you can never go back, sometimes it really is too late.

Like death.

Like life.

*

I was born out of necessity. My mother told me she'd been pushed into a corner she did not want to stand in. At a parish dance, at the back of the hall, she ruffled up her pleated skirt and crossed her arms over her chest. She was made up to the nines and in love with Bill Haley and his skyward Comets. She knew everything about him she possibly could and daydreamed of being at one of his concerts, staring up into his face as he sang to her, noticing her above all the others. She was twenty-three, her cheeks rouged and lips painted, full to overbrimming. She liked to boast about Bill Haley, about all the information she had amassed on him. In the back of her mind, she had even fancied that one night he would come to the parish dance and they would fall in love, a love at first sight.

My father would walk round the hall, one hand sewn deep into his pocket, the other holding a cigarette. He smoked American cigarettes. My father, Tom Pogue with black, greased-back hair and drain-pipes, skirting the perimeter, looking at the girls all dandified and peacock pretty, and he stopped beside my mother and asked her to dance.

Tom Pogue was a natural dancer, all the women said so, they said he had the look of a Hollywood movie star. He agreed, he was off to America to become one, just as soon as he got the money together, he'd be on the boat and away. My mother wrapped in his arms and they danced together the whole of the night and he looked into her eyes and imagined she was Ginger Rogers and she looked into his and thought who needs Bill Haley.

Twirling in and out, till the band packed up and already they were an item, the pair of them walked hand in hand back to her home and he kissed her under the stars as a curtain fluttered lightly in the window by the door.

A monthly parish dance and as the months passed by my mother's jitterbug improved no end. Her heels wore thin and everyone was speculating about when Tom would make it official and sweep my mother off her feet. Tom with his wild dreams, a star in the making, if he got the chance, if he saved real hard. If . . .

He'd say Ginger and Fred better watch out, there'll be havoc in Hollywood all right and they won't know what hit them.

Together they'd walk home and sometimes they would stall awhile to dance beneath the flickering lights of the night sky. He would hold her close, his hand tight around her waist, pulling her into him, to the music playing on in their heads.

Then there I was on the Dundrum road, on the way to my first death.

It was high summer and I cannot have been more than two foot in length. My mother stood behind me, pushing me along towards the light that made my eyes squint. She was humming a song, a song I heard many times but could not sing for the words had yet to formulate within. See it was during that period of senses, sounds and differing shades of light.

I liked that time, when everything was new.

My hands clasped at the small rail in front, as my mother's heels slapped the pavement at a brisk pace. I had pushed aside the coloured plastic shapes to make room for my pudgy fingers clenched around the rail and was rocking back and forth slightly. I used to think this motion helped our overall movement, my mother mistook it for some form of primitive dance and raised her voice with renewed vigour. I jolted, my mother halted the buggy to a stop and was hollering across the street to what I perceived as an almost mirror image. A woman on a kerbside, hollering, stood next to a buggy like mine. We crossed, our chairs placed together, our mothers bent over to examine and confirm that their own was the more beautiful, perfect or whatever and finding so, relieved, they struck up a conversation.

'America you say, that's an awful long way,' exclaimed my mother.

'His brother is there, says there's plenty jobs and what with things as they are over here, we thought it only best.'

'You're right for sure. I heard Maud's Jonno was laid off last week and she's got three kiddies. When are you off?'

'A week on Sunday, can't begin to tell you what a load there is to be sorted. How's Tom?'

'Same as ever, working at the post office, in a very good position. He'll up that ladder in no time at all. Mark my words.'

We separated shortly after our mothers had blessed each other. God blessing, not a sneeze in sight. Take care now and the best of luck, promising to keep in touch.

We were on our way to the butchers. I had not been to a butchery before or if I had, I had never noticed.

There was a pig hanging in the window, its sides split open, its trotters suspended as if it had shed its skin and brought upon its own demise. My mother picked out some choice pieces of meat and we turned around to retrace our steps.

Back home I sat in my highchair, playing aeroplanes. My father spooning journeys into my mouth. Pureed and innocent, my mother standing close by, frying up his steak.

'All the way to America,' and I opened wide, swallowed the destination as she turned the ladle in her hand and says to him,

'You'll never guess who I bumped into today.'

'What's that?'

'Margaret Cochane. You remember we used to work together at the Exchange.'

'Is that so.'

'I told you about her I'm sure of it, well isn't she only married with a kiddie and another on the way. And aren't they only going off to live in America.'

'Is that right?'

'She didn't say, but I expect her man hasn't worked in an age. Her coat was in tatters and the baby dressed in rags.'

'Good luck to them.'

'That's what I said.'

One day I would go to this America.

Star-spangled country, the land of dreams. Sleepy head, to slumber there, and shroud myself in a blanket of stars.

Nine months after they tied themselves in knots, I'd arrived. Nineteen years later I left.

'Gee that's really moving,' sympathized Dot. 'Though you didn't have to go into so much detail.' Extracting a tissue from the end of her sleeve she wiped her headset, a little ritual she did every night before switching on.

'Sorry,' I apologized, 'I was on a roll, you know how it is.'

'Never mind it'll probably work to your advantage in this place.'

Aware I'd hogged the conversation I returned the favour. Her present quandary concerned whether she should ditch her boyfriend Fred or marry him.

'I mean I love him, I do love him, he's a swell guy. But . . .'

'What?'

'I have certain misgivings. I don't know but every time I marry, it falls apart. Maybe I should just skip that stage and then maybe we'll stay together.'

Dot had been married twice already. She was only twenty-five.

'Well third time lucky.'

'Yeah Fred's real sweet, he's a good guy.'

Dot was sweet too, lipsmacking delicious. She was really good on the phones and managed to drum in about twice the amount of business as anyone else. We swapped leads for luck. She filled me in on all the tricks of the trade.

Retirees and single mothers were rated the best. The aim being to frighten the wits out of them. See they'd chat to you, would tell you their whole life story, how many kids, husbands, lovers, pets they had, their house plans, social lives, alarm systems, their utter vulnerability. It was easy, they'd spill the beans and it was left to us to go in and empty their coffers.

'Ma'am we'd like to point out that double glazing is very safe, I mean you can't just open up a window, like the one you have in your front room at the moment.'

'I'm telling you ma'am you wouldn't even hear the bastards next door.'

'How precious is your security? Think of the child. Exactly how much can you afford not to spend on your own safety?'

'Excuse me sir, but the amount of winter heat that just drains away, think how toasty warm you would be, it would do your arthritis such good. Hey is that the sound of your bones unwinding or a tingle on the line.'

A tingle on the line.

It had gone seven, I was just about to go on break.

I picked up the receiver, this was odd, the phones hardly ever rang. Personal calls were prohibited, a sackable offence and everyone in the office turned their eyes on me.

'You're through to Clear Glazers, how can I help?'

'Hi is that Murrey? It's Man . . .'

'Double glazing sir,' I shouted to reassure my co-workers.

'I see, well I'd like to buy some double glazing please.'

Lowering my voice to a whisper, 'Are you kidding me?'

'Would I ring if I was?'

'Sir, you could be a crank caller and then where would I be? See at Clear Glazers Co. we make the calls. Actually you are technically speaking meant to have had one of our salesmen call round to your house, ply you with pamphlets outlining why you should choose Clear Glazers Co. and then when you are registered on our data system we call you. We are a reputable company, there are no cold calls. Do you understand?'

'Sure,' but he persevered, 'I'm interested in double glazing, I'd like to know more about it.'

He gave me his number and I told him I'd call him straight back. Let off the hook, it was a play to redivert my colleagues' attention. As long as I didn't veer too far from the script it'd work. I dialled his digits.

'Hi this is Murrey, I'm calling on behalf of Clear Glazers Company, we deal in double glazing would you be interested?'

He said it really wasn't his thing.

'It's not really my thing but you can tell me a little about it.'

'Clear Glazers was set up in 1996 by a couple of wide boys who realized there was a corner market, in a corner market, to logistically fob people off with crap merchandise, while at the same time extolling its virtues. The two guys in question, a Marty Spegal and a Darius Wurster are respectively assholes of the dirtiest type. Basically as kids they used to amuse themselves by making crank calls, the usual adolescent shit, ordering pizzas for people who didn't want them, taxis, mail order goods, prostitutes. Anyhow they soon got bored and started extorting money out of people they didn't know or care about and eventually they were traced. The upshot being, neither of them can talk to anyone face to face and they need always to be on the phone in order to relate to anyone or anything. Clear Glazers is one of a hundred companies they run and because it was their first, they tend to hold it dear to them. Also it is the most mainstream of the lot, or morally acceptable.'

'Hmm what are you up to later?'

'Clear Glazers offers the purchaser two panes of glass for the price of one. Yes and I can hear you already thinking, wow what a great deal.' (This was all part of the spiel). 'Two for one. Why it must be a bargain.'

'And is it a bargain?'

'According to the script it is. Yes, I'd like that. Two for the price of one. That's right sir, two whole panes of glass for the price of one.'

'How many times do you have to repeat that phrase?'

'It's a form of indoctrination. You know repetition, expect your caller to have no more than one brain cell. It's imperative to keep repeating the name of the company and the bargain side of the product.'

'If you're free it'd be nice to see you but go on with the hard sell.'

'Clear Glazers Co. was set up in 1996 . . .'

'You've already said that.'

'Oh yeah sorry, I lost my place and my shift's just started. Okay so not only do you get two for the price of one, but we take out your old windows and replace them with Clear Glazers' double sheen, soundproof, windproof, ageproof, smashproof, a hundred per cent proof.'

'Proof of what?' he asked.

'That you'll see more out of a Clear Glazers window than you ever saw before.'

'How do you make that out?'

'Well for a start you'll be seeing double.'

'And how much will all this cost?'

'Sir we don't pretend to come cheap. We're no fly-by-night dealers. We will still be here the next morning if you need to call us. We make no bones about it, we are a quality-driven company. Bargains are for cheap-skates. If you are a cheapskate then put the phone down now,' I paused for a few seconds. 'Sir if you are one of those people always looking for the cheapest price, then I urge you to hang up,' again I paused. 'If indeed sir, you are a low individual who cuts corners, we will give you the number of another glazers intent on ripping you off and doing your windows for half the price we do them.'

This being another company owned by the inestimable dorks I worked for.

'So how much does it cost?'

'How much the price of clarity my good friend. How much the price of a clear conscience, you tell me.'

He told me where he lived and asked that I call by with some more information. I said I'd have to check with my supervisor, that his request was rather unethical. I didn't want to labour the point or get jobsworthy but the terms in my contract categorically stated I was to sell via the phone, not face to face. There was a whole other script for that.

'It's obviously not a good time.'

No time like the present and I urged him to hang on.

'Fine I'll wait.'

I gestured to Dot that I had a real livewire on the line and went in search of Martha our supervisor.

'Martha there's some guy on the line who lives in a mansion and wants me to go round with information about Clear Glazers.'

'A mansion, well maybe I should deal with him.'

Martha was huge, she carried her arse round with her and I wondered how difficult it was for her to move, she had nine kids and I was perplexed how it had been possible in the first place. No one seemed to like her, they were all scared shitless of her.

She straddled over to my desk and started speaking to my lead.

Obviously I couldn't hear what he was saying, only her side of the story.

'You see our operatives are not required to make

house calls . . . Achem, really well . . . Yes I see but I could . . . Yes of course . . . Well thank you very much . . . Yes that's correct, two for the price of one.'

She put down the receiver, 'Grab yourself a taxi girl and don't blow it.'

I stepped out of the office and a taxi pulled up, right in front of me. So easy, fitting into place and I thought this is destiny, destiny awaits. The driver, a Portuguese kid, wore a baseball cap and was dressed in white. She drove with one hand on the wheel looking back at me every couple of seconds, bypassing the rearview mirror.

'Know what ladee you look real . . . well do I know you?'

I told her I'd been around a bit, so it was possible, though I couldn't recall having met her.

'I know what it is, you remind me of my cousin Jolita.'

I leant forward, 'Really?'

'Spitting image.'

'What's she like then?'

'Dead.'

'Oh.'

'Yep, nasty death lady. Real nasty.'

And though I didn't want to push the point, I did.

'How'd it happen?'

'She was a bus driver, our whole family's in transport. She had a good route, you know, not too many crazy areas, picking up mainly kiddies and domestics. Anyways she's driving along, minding her own business, letting on the kiddies . . .'

Interrupting her, I gushed, 'Don't tell me, a kid takes out an Uzi and guns her dead.'

'Nah they all loved her, she was like a mother to some of those kiddies. Listen to me, it was just another ordinary day picking up the Filipino women . . .'

'I get it, menopausal hara-kiri, takes the wheel of the bus, drives into a wall, smashing her to smithereens.'

'No lady, those women were her best friends. She played poker with them Tuesday nights, they'd bet hours of cleaning. One week she had to give up driving the bus, she lost so bad. Anyhows she's driving along . . . you know she used to sweat a lot, I remember the smell of her, it just used to fall out of her. As I say she's driving through the projects and a group of young guys get on. You know the type, muthafuckas raging with attitude.'

'I know, I know!!' My hand shooting upward, like when I was in class. 'They gang rape her to death?'

'No way ladee, these guys are loyal, she's been picking them up since they were kiddies themselves. You sure are a sick individual.'

'Well you said a horrible death.'

'Yeah, so listen, she finishes her shift, drives the bus back to the station, goes has a drink with the guys at work. And like she likes her drink, you know she likes her drink. Anyhows she's walking home and stops by the corner store to get something or other, when a guy walks in to rob the place. Fuck knows what happens, but she's shot, like shot dead. That's D. E. A. D. You know?'

'Dog,' I said.

'Worse, them people are worse than animals. Scum.'

'So when did this happen?'

'Last night.'

'Christ.' I didn't really know what to say after that.

'Yeah, you remind me of her a little.'

'Thanks.'

She pulled over to the kerbside, 'This here is the address.'

'Great, hope I get you again,' I said, struggling out of the car and I gave her a generous tip, felt obliged.

Sure he lived in a mansion, a mansion block but then again, maybe he was the landlord and wanted to do up all the windows. Jee that got me thinking, all that commission, I could retire, I'd be a millionaire, wouldn't have to play the Lotto anymore. I could stuff my face with chocolates, eat till I got sick and then employ a fitness instructor to ease it all off. I pressed his buzzer, 1147, and he asked who it was.

'I'm from Clear Glazers,' I answered.

'Look it's the top floor, sorry but the elevator's out of order.'

'You could have told me before I left the office. I would have worn my hiking boots.'

He didn't laugh.

This was a good sign cause it wasn't funny.

I counted each floor, he lived on the fourteenth, but really the thirteenth, you know how some buildings omit to name the thirteenth floor. My legs were jelly and his door was open and I pushed it aside and walked in.

He had a panoramic view of the whole city, it was breathtaking, obviously there was no possible way we could double glaze this.

'Hello I'm here, I made it.'

I couldn't see him. Come out, come out, from wherever you are?

Then, what do you know, only . . .

He walked down into the room holding a couple of steaming mugs in his hands, cupping them in his palms.

'You must be cold,' he said.

'Freezing, it's freezing out there.' He walked toward to me and I took a mug from out of his hand, raised it to my lips to sip the contents, orange ginger lemon and honey. Yummy.

'Thanks, you've a great place here.'

'Yeah, so what do you think?'

'Well, I'm not sure we at Clear Glazers can do anything for you. Are you married?' I blurted it out.

'Why do you ask?'

I had to.

'It's just . . . mostly we sell to couples. Old or young couples, it tends to be our main market. One of the lines in the script categorically states that we must determine the status of the potential buyer within the opening minutes of the conversation. Have you lived here long?'

'Five years.'

'Where were you before?'

'Montreal, have you been there?'

'No.'

He asked how I'd ended up in Chicago.

'You sure you want to know?'

'Yeah, I'm interested,' came the reply.

'Certain?' I practically cautioned him, drew in a humongous breath and was about to exhale when Dot's pained expression haunted my mind. Stood by the window, the teeming city below, I offered an abbreviated version and he listened, appeared genuinely interested. Then, having finished my drink, he took me on a tour of his apartment. He showed me all the views, pointed out the buildings he liked.

'On the corner down there to the left is an Italian restaurant, I sometimes eat there on a Thursday, a saxophonist comes by to play for his supper, I think you may like it.'

Was that an offer?

We talked some more, I said it was good to have met again and wondered why it had taken so long. He smiled, asked what I thought of the book. I told him it was just beginning to get good, I was just beginning to get into it, had almost reached halfway. He laughed a little and I told him his lips were full and wide, like a woman's.

He mentioned he had something for me and to wait, while he went to get it. I sat in his armchair, looking about the room.

'They'll have to go,' I shouted down the hallway to him.

'What will?' he cried back.

'Those two paintings.'

'You reckon?'

'Sure they're passé and devoid of any truthful emotion.'

I heard him holler, 'Got it,' then requested I shut my eyes. 'Are your eyes closed?'

'No they're wide open.'

'Well close them.'

'No way,' I replied. 'I'm not a complete fool. Sure you could be the latest maniac everyone is talking about, who lures young innocents up to his apartment on the pretence of . . . rstuvwxyz.'

'I don't get you,' he sounded confused.

'Well, of making a huge commission.'

'Then what happens?'

'Okay so you intoxicate them with some herbal drink, making sure the elevator is out of order cause then they have even less chance of escape. Next you say, "I've got something for you," and you wander off down the hallway to get your strangling string and on your return, you ask the victim to close their eyes and then you pounce.'

'So for the last time, are your eyes closed?'

'Yeah,' I called back.

I could hear his approaching steps. Thud, thud, the heavy, steady sound of his breath (which, he claimed, was due to a nasty head cold) while I held mine and he crouched down by me and wrapped my scarf about my neck.

Glad to have it back, I drew the soft velvety material across my face. 'Thanks, thanks for keeping it for me.'

'Pleasure,' and he looked at me askance, 'Are you okay?'

I shuddered, reckoned I'd freaked myself out.

'I better be going or the supervisor will hit the roof,' I explained. 'Do you think you'll bother with the double glazing?'

'I'll think about it some more,' he answered.

I handed him the literature I had brought with.

'I want you . . .' I said, looking into his eyes.

'Pardon me?'

'I want you to read the pamphlet and let me know what you think.'

I asked him to chaperone me down the stairs and caught a cab back to the office.

Dot asked me what he was like.

'Don't know.'

I mean he seemed really nice.

Martha interrogated me on whether I had sold him on the idea.

I couldn't really say. He said he'd ring next week.

'Next week,' she screamed, 'Next fucking week? He was winding us up. If he dares ring again, just put him on to me.'

Unaware of his pursuit, I had not envisaged such a turn of events but then life is like that, it has a habit of creeping up on you, surprising you from behind and stabbing you through the heart. But of that and what was to occur, I was still safe in my ignorance. I had not thought of it, for it did not occur to me, lost in my own pursuit, that I, myself could be pursued.

It could have been scripted what was to happen. That initial glance, an immediate pull. Yes, in retrospect I had acquired a taste, the soothing essence of ginger honey lay on my tongue. I went home that night and bathed for hours till my skin crinkled, not just the tips of my fingers, my whole body wrinkled. As I dried myself in front of the mirror, I saw myself aged and thought of my mother.

Dear Ma

Tonight I am warm. I am warm and wet and thawing.

I have not thought of you for a while, for my head has been empty, my tongue grew lazy and flapped uneasily in my mouth, there has been nothing to say for so long, so I have not written.

Do you ever get like that?

Irony is I have ended up travelling the Mother Road. Criss-crossed the country like a demented soul to arrive in Chicago a few months ago and if you'd asked me, did I know where I was headed, I wouldn't have had an answer. I was in a state after state; sunflower, golden, lone star . . . On the road travelling down that line of intermittent pauses, only in reverse, like an upside down 99.

Chicawgo and I like it here, huge but manageable, with a lake like a sea and what was once the tallest building in the world. Even got myself a job, officially lying to people. Well you were always telling me I was prone to exaggerate, so I cod them into buying double glazing.

Will you send me your recipe for drop scones? I miss the melting taste. Is our home as warm as I imagine it. Do you remember the time I made you cry?

Sorry.

Murrey

WHEN Manfredi asked how old she was, she said she stopped counting at seven.

He walked her to the door, down the fourteen flights and waited for a cab to show, listening as she babbled on.

'I thought I'd lost you, haven't seen you round for a while,' she confessed, wrapping her scarf round her neck and tucking wisps of hair back, beneath her hat.

'Know what?' She was looking up into his face.

'What?'

'Your lips they're just like a woman's.'

She had stayed over an hour. Wayward talking of everything and nothing. Manfredi asked how she'd ended up in Chicago and she described how she'd got the train.

'Yeah I like the train and it was weird cause I never talk to strangers. I mean it's just something I don't do.

I was seated beside this guy dressed in a white suit. You
know like some mercy angel. I thought he'd been sent
to save me or maybe even kidnap me.'

She swooped off on a tangent launching into an
episode about how she'd become entangled with
some neo-religious, Christian fundamentalists, before
eventually working her way back to the train
compartment.

'Totally in white; I mean shoes, socks, suit, shirt, the
lot. And he leant towards me and said, what's your
name and where do you come from? I felt like I was a
contestant on a game show and looked around for a
hidden camera, just in case I was being monitored. You
know, *Candid Camera*, or if it was a set up. You can
never be too careful. Anyhow we got talking and he
confided, he was looking for someone. Aren't we all I
said. "Not like this," he admitted, declared he was
after someone, said he couldn't rest until he'd found
this person or quenched himself of this personal
torment. The long and short of it was . . .'

She stopped and looked up at Manfredi.

'I can't remember why I'm telling you this story.'

She paused to think over what she had said, took a
few moments to reflect. 'Oh yeah, coming to Chicago.
See I'm really interested in architecture and that was
the initial reason. You know, all the truly great
buildings they have here. As I kid, I used to believe if
you stood on the top floor of the tallest building in the
world you'd be able to reach out and yank a star down
from the heavens. So the very first thing I did when I
arrived here was race to the Sears Tower and ride the
express elevator up to the hundred and third floor.

'Can't tell you how sick I felt when I reached the top.
My head all oozy and legs shaky. I mean it was such a

disappointment, the fact that it's no longer the tallest building.' She sighed, her head shaking, 'Sorry I always do this, go off on one, sorry.'

Manfredi sat listening, intrigued, carried away on her banter. 'And the man in the carriage?' he prompted her.

'The man dressed in white. You know, he never did tell me his name but he leant toward me and asked if I had anywhere to stay and, if I didn't, he knew of a vacant apartment. I'm pretty confident he was okay but you can never be certain, so I thanked him and said sure, that'd be cool. We kept chatting, right up until the train pulled into the station. I got my bags, he got his, we said goodbye and then remembering his offer, he wrote down the address on a red flick matchbox for me . . . Shit what time is it?'

She realized she'd been babbling over an hour and said she had to get back or they'd be worried at the office, think he was some freak.

Manfredi wanted to know the end of her story, what, if anything, had happened.

'Oh no nothing,' she replied, 'I must have chucked the matchbox in the trashcan by mistake. It was a real pain in the ass, cause as a consequence I've had to stay in a flea pit.'

Manfredi looked blankly at her, like he'd missed the point.

'Now I remember. The thing is I have this weird suspicion, the address on the matchbox was for a flat in this very building . . . Isn't that strange. I mean isn't it spooky?'

It wasn't until she left, till the moment when, retracing his steps back up to his apartment, it occurred to

Manfredi they were, to all purposes, complete strangers. He hadn't bent forward to kiss her when they parted, just fleetingly touched her face. Seven and he laughed aloud. She'd made him laugh.

I DON'T doubt there is ever any point in diving head first into a delicate situation, especially when the chances are you could do yourself some serious coronary damage.

So I forced myself to return momentarily into the shadows and relish every inch of the journey about to be embarked upon. I hummed and hawed, huffed and puffed for all of a day, then overcome by a massive desire to stuff my face with pasta, I decided to try out the Italian restaurant.

Was that an offer?

On the safe side I called Dot, asking if herself and Fred fancied dinner. Manzoni's and I imagined chequered tablecloths and jugs of wine, a fine fat momma behind the bar and her beautiful daughter taking orders. Red paper napkins and meaty bolognese, sash-curtained windows with the menu nailed to the door outside, *casa, casa* and that's exactly how it was.

Red candles on the table, breadsticks in waxy paper, I caught sight of Fred and Dot sitting in the corner and went to join them.

We ordered a carafe of red wine and after a glass or two I saw Manfredi enter. I'd been fiddling with the table candle, listening to Fred long-wind about his dodgy gut. The wax had softened and I was spilling it on to the tips of my fingers, making a mess, when I noticed him. My heart jumped my mouth and I didn't feel like eating at all.

Manfredi greeted the owner with a kiss, either side of her cheeks. A waiter took his coat and then the coat of his companion. He was with another woman. I recognized her from Al's and waved over to them, wax-tipped fingers, a burning sensation.

'You made it,' he said.

'Yeah thanks, it's always good to find somewhere new.' Flushed in the face, yet thankful the words came out.

Manfredi introduced himself and Debra, I introduced Fred and Dot. They joined our table and I was pushed to the edge. It wasn't meant to be like this, for I felt like a gooseberry disturbing a foursome. Physically he was twice removed from me and I noticed he wanted anchovies on his pizza. I ordered the same.

The conversation lagged, spluttering between mouthfuls and the evening seemed to flounder, unbalanced, until the saxophonist struck up a chord to mellow us out. Then Manfredi came and sat by me, while Debra got up to dance alone.

Sat beside each other, quietly listening to those blue notes of the saxophonist bellow forth. In rhythm with the music tapping his hand on his raised right leg. He looked happy. The pair of us batting sidelong glances. Then Dot was pulled up on to the small platform, Fred urging her to sing. Dot rose to the occasion as everyone's attention swung round to her. She was showing off.

'Your friend has a great voice,' Manfredi commented.

'I sing too,' I said.

'Come here,' he took me by the hand and led me to the dancefloor. By now Fred was dancing with Debra.

'I can't dance,' I protested.

'Just follow me,' and I closed my eyes.

*

'I can't dance,' I squealed and there I was, decked out in a maxi dress, hair in ringlets with my mother telling me not to be making a show of myself. Aunt Nora's wedding, the groom, that no-good Archie. Descended, my mother informed me, from pig breed. I had gone straight up to the high table. Was it true, was Archie a pig like my mother said?

Caught staring up at him.

'What you looking for Murrey?'

'Your snout,' just like my mother had said, only he laughed raising a pint glass up at her, then belched with a fierce power while she beamed puce. Told you so, in heaven's name, can't you keep your mouth shut? Skipping merrily back to within her grasp and spitting range and she grabbed my wrist, twisting it hard to make sure it was connected properly. Wait till I get you home, the words came snaking out of her mouth. Why, I wondered. Why? And my father was laughing.

Last time I saw him laughing. You little devil, and the band strikes up. Archie and Nora took to the floor, the hem of her dress caught beneath the leg of a chair, throwing her up in the air and everyone erupting with the laughter.

'See if yous can do any better,' cried Archie helping Nora up, the bridesmaids fluttering about, fixing the tiara she had stuck to her head, while the band played on.

'Come on and we'll dance,' says my father.

'I can't dance,' so I stand on his toes, balancing and off we go, round and round and before long there is a small crowd gathered, egging us on cause he's pulling me any which way, swinging me over his shoulder, sliding me under his legs and up again. I was loving it, in fits and starts of giggles and when the music stopped there was a round of applause. I curtsied and ran back to the table, 'Did you see me Mum?' My father followed.

'You have her ruined,' she says.

'You have her ruined,' I mimic and again, because I'm a child and she's an adult.

'Stop it Murrey.'

'Stop it Murrey.' I mimic, and again because I'm a child and she's an adult.

She whacks me one, I burst out crying.

I protested, 'I can't dance.' Manfredi wasn't listening, he held me close and when Dot sang the last note, I lifted up my face, and he kissed me on the forehead.

I opened my eyes, discovered his weren't even closed.

He kissed me on the forehead. I'd wanted him to kiss me on the lips. This was what I noticed and that he had brought that woman Debra with him.

We paid the bill and left shortly after.

Dot said to me the next day at work, she said she thought Manfredi was into me.

I wasn't sure, uncertain of how to read him, my mood had changed and I was feeling unsettled.

MANFREDI had kissed her on the forehead. He should have kissed her on the lips. When they danced, she kept treading on his toes, her eyes closed and face turned into his chest.

Alone in the studio, he kept picking up the phone then replacing it, found himself procrastinating between sudden bursts of energy, yet unable to concentrate on any specific thing for more than an hour. Submerged in an excruciating wave of self-consciousness, he aimed to avoid any fuck-ups and jerk forward in the wrong direction. Timing was all important.

Forty-eight hours had passed since their meeting at the restaurant. There was nothing worse than appearing too eager, too needy. Desperate. He tried in vain to censor his thoughts but they meandered and focused on her. Her scent, face, body, the energy she carried about her and all the while thinking perhaps . . . perhaps, not sure what to expect, so better not to.

The phone rang, he picked it up.

Straight off she asked, 'Why haven't you rung me?'

She had beaten him to it.

He answered, 'I was just thinking of calling.'

'Truthfully?'

'Swear to you.'

The phone went dead. He waited a few seconds in case she'd been cut off, then he picked up the receiver and called Clear Glazers.

'Hey it's me.'

'Me who?'

'Manfredi.'

'Sir at Clear Glazers we pride ourselves on the level of service and attention to detail we offer. I can assure you now, before either of us waste any more time, you will not be disappointed. Do you understand?'

'Yeah, you can't talk right now.'

'Sir let me put it like this. It's time to make a decision.'

'You were right,' he answered, 'I don't think it would work.'

'Sorry, excuse me but can you repeat that please? I think I misheard.'

'The double glazing,' he said, 'I'm not convinced. What do you think?'

'Loads of things, they stream through me. How come you brought Debra with the other night?'

'Debra, she's an old friend, works in Al's. She's going out with the saxophonist.'

'I get you, it's just I don't like crossing my wires or getting the wrong end of the stick.'

'Sure I understand.'

'So sir and I'm not one for the heavy sale but I urge you to reconsider, double glazing can be very beneficial.'

'Convince me.'

'I shouldn't have to, you should just feel it.'

He laughed.

'Look,' he said, 'I have a house up by the lake, the windows are all rotting, maybe you should come up and have a look.'

Gulping back every word, Manfredi hadn't anticipated inviting Murrey away, it just came out. Nor had he planned on taking a holiday but then again the season was about to commence and no obstacles stood in his way. There was no reason not to go, his subconscious had made itself heard. A grin etched deeply on his face and, throat dry, Manfredi contemplated how strange their dance towards one another had been, like a pinball shooting off to strike it lucky.

He left Chicago a couple of days later, took a train up to a holiday home he shared with friends.

The place, a simple cabin of painted white, slated timber, lay close to a small fishing village on the eastern-shore of Lake Michigan, lying empty since the summer. Manfredi arrived in advance, to get it in order and rid it of the musty smell of dampness.

SOMETIMES you just got to trust your intuition and take a chance.

And that was definitely an offer.

Sat on the train, as field follows field, as the light lessened and cast a gloom in the wintry compartment. I was hiding out in the first-class carriage, it was empty and warm. I pressed my cheeks against the cool glass, my thoughts flowing freely with the meditative motion of the train, staring out the window and drowsed, eyes half shut. As the train drew to a standstill, I didn't doubt for a moment he wouldn't show. I was squinting at an angle, my neck strained, as far as it could go, just so I could see him. Stood on the platform, shifting from foot to foot, looking at the clock, the jerking minute-hand had just touched six. The train expected in view, the guard pacing the platform.

Manfredi was waiting for me.

I could not suppress the smile taking over my face and he stood tall and lean with those curls unfurling untidily about his face. He looked cold and hesitant. I wondered if he was nervous. That blue scarf around his neck and he was peering in at the carriages, to see which one I would appear from.

I was feeling open, ceased thinking, touched down.

Then hit by a blast of icy coldness, almost choking, I heaved my bag on to the platform and turned to see him walk towards me.

There always seems to be such distance in those last few paces.

Passed recognizing one another but not quite met.

'Sorry,' I muttered.

'Pardon?'

'Nothing, it's pre-emptive,' I explained, 'I mean it just slipped out.'

He gave me a hug and told me I was welcome. Carried my bag for me, already a weight off my shoulders, and he asked what I had brought with. Emotion I sighed inward and then we passed through the small station out to the car park. He had a large rust estate car and he told me it was an old family one. 'The house,' he said, 'it's real simple, I hope I haven't misled you and you're expecting some grand place.' He heaved my bag into the back seat of the car. I sat in the front, it was cold, clapping together my gloved hands and blowing my breath into them. He pulled the safety belt across him.

Too late, I thought as the engine started up.

Chit-chatting and it was his turn to babble and he told me stuff about his family, how as a kid he and his dad had won fishing championships three years in a row, fly fishing, he liked to fish but hadn't for years not since his father's death.

Listening hard and I sought to look beyond his words, to decipher what he was really saying. I had this urge to reach out and lay my hand over his.

He told me the place was an hour's drive.

Wide roads, straight and narrow, we were going all the way.

Sat, side-sneaking glimpses and already I wanted to dance with him, to move with him.

Then suddenly we were off the beaten track, cracking gravel as his foot rested easy on the brake in front of the house. It was timber layered, curtain comfort from the cold and the fire stoked. It was perfect.

'I'll draw back the drapes tomorrow, to check the panes,' I intimated.

He laughed, agreed it would be best.

'You must be tired after all that travelling.'

My head nodded in accordance.

I left my bags at the top of the stairs on the landing, didn't want to tempt fate too much. It was thick pitch outside and a fire smouldered in the hearth. I showered, reawakening my senses, dulled by travelling, into a state of somnolence. Changed into a clean pair of jeans and soft jumper. I let my hair hang loose to my shoulders, then went downstairs and found Manfredi in the kitchen, cooking supper and listening to some jazz.

He smiled as I wandered through.

'Feel better?'

'Mmm.' Momentarily wordless and I sat by the edge of the wooden kitchen table watching him, my hand gripped around a wineglass stem, to steady myself, as we glanced at one another, surprised by our respective presences.

And I can't for the life of me think what we talked about during that uncomfortable time, as we inched towards one another . . .

. . . then there I was . . .

Swept up in him, sat on the porch, starry eyed, mouth to mouth, words passing from the tip of my tongue, to his and he told me all about himself and I told him all about himself.

Manfredi, Manfredi, Monday, Tuesday, Wednesday, Thursday.

Amber eyes and he held my hand as we walked along the pathway, down to the lakeside shore.

*

It happened simple as that.

To flute like follow on a passionate note of understanding as there is no alternative and giving up is
giving everything and more natural than breathing in
sync beside her to glide above her, move moth-like
towards her as nakedly unconscious he took her to bed
to kiss constant mouth to mouth and human resus-
citation, his hands upon her softness and all over
touching as much paleness as possible to be caught in
a high-tide wave of emotion, of skin-tight thigh, hip,
buttock, back, belly, neck, foot, free fall into her and
she devouring as he eases inside and further for she
tugs at him, clutches and greedy pulls at him tightly, his
body covering hers beneath, and still his lips upon her,
clenched in one long-held solid breath, of sense and
sensuality of smell and deep pungent odour, over,
under, gently, forceful, love is slow, quick quick, slow
. . . to slumber ache and recognize mortality and life
consecutively at the same time, so rare it works so well,
so sweetly damp and moist and drenched in one
another, a changing charging rhythm, it is the only
truth warmwetdryhardsoftmuskbreath and again and
once more and every other experience diminishes to
real surrender. He comes into her as she covers him
and they remain soft panting drifting through the night
back to one another and he looks upon her and thinks
how beautiful she is and kisses her softly, stirring her,
stroking her. And he caresses her face as she falls asleep
and watches to see a hint of her dreams.

This dream recurring, which I have carried with me

since childhood, begins with a woman, born almost raw, who follows me as a shadow, or I, her.

At that precise moment when I surrender to sleep, she appears. In silhouette against eye drapes she looms, ready to embark upon her nocturnal quest to find a skin she can slip into and warm her heart. Guided by this sole preoccupation, she has travelled far and wide and such is her determination she is quite unable to remain still. Her lips tremble in anticipation and at times her eyes mist over to shroud her vision.

Unfortunately, the latter has led her to experience countless false sightings and minor discrepancies and as a result she has suffered a mounting sense of frustration.

Oftentimes I have dreamt of her and not once has she ever given up hope and though every dream took her someplace new, it would always end the same way.

Mile after mile is trod till she walks barefoot, her shoes soul shod and her floral patterned dress worn thin. Its flowers lie deadened on the fabric, the petals fallen to its hem, yet nevertheless she perseveres. Onward she goes, till indeed her bones protrude through tightly drawn skin, tight as a drum so that every heartbeat reverberates inside. How she aches, she aches so much and realizing something is going to give, she decides to meet it head on, climbs up on a soapbox at the corner of a street and screams.

'We are living in an age and that is all I can tell you. You may call me a crank and that may be true.'

The empty streets echo a small round of silent applause, urging her on.

'My dreams, I do not remember for they are borne into reality, they are as real as existence.'

And with every bit of strength left within, she declares.

'What is a remembered dream but an image fragment, hurtling through your mind's eye. We are all of us silent, screaming, toothless, falling, ever falling, cruising aimlessly to a full stop. Wake up call and again motion going through, to sustain something akin to a hope.'

She takes a deep breath, continuing with her nonsense,

'To go on journeys of discovery bringing you back to square one, familiarity. We crab it side to side. No one ever talks of square two. See no one ever talks of square two. To everything you ever fled from, how long can you flee? I am tired of trying. Where is my only dream, my sustenance, the reason I wake each morning?'

'Not so far, I smelt him on the sidewalk only yesterday.'

'Who said that?'

A downtrodden roadsweeper emerges from the shadows and calls out to her.

'Go to hell with your ranting.'

Unperturbed she forces the issue,

'What direction was he going in?'

He points the bristle end of the brush outward and immediately she sets off in the given direction just as the light of the dawn breaks through.

Usually I wake at this point, but that night lying beside Manfredi I dreamt on. His steady breathing, soothing against the back of my neck and curled around me as a form of protection.

For the first time ever the dream proceeded.

*

132

She with her skin so translucent, continued on in the direction given by the irksome roadsweeper. She walked to the end of the summer, through autumn, indeed till winter caught up on her again. Then struck by the season she slowed down, allowing herself to feel the cold and it was then that she paused, finding herself a huge distance from her initial starting point.

Down a dirt-track on a road to nowhere, standing stock still and she failed to notice a character come charging towards her. Steadfast in his strides, he blundered forward and looking beyond his presence, they collided. The stranger insistent, persistent clung to her arm as she staggered backward and it was twenty metres or more before she realized they had become entangled.

Thus forced to jolt, halt with her arm wrapped around him, she turned to him, as he did her.

She caught him by the scruff of his neck, her arm entwined and gave him the once, twice over. Eye, eye, from the corner of, and he looked somewhat familiar. He said.

'You look somewhat familiar.'

'You do,' she agreed.

'Do you know me?'

'As much as I know you.'

And at the every same instant they both cried out,

'I have a strange feeling I may have met you before,' and they laughed at their similarities.

Then she, with her eyes so large, her vision distorted, blink blinked, their faces moving together and untangling from him, she noticed his peculiarity. He was dressed in white as perhaps an innocent would be. All in white, from his shoes to his cravat but for the most preposterous of sights, for pinned slightly to the left side of his chest was his heart. Yes he displayed his heart quite openly, as if ready to give it to the first person he should bump into.

This is what occurred to her as she felt the colour rush into her.

Every step worth treading, and a feeling implanted in her subconscious was borne into reality, as a strain of life or some such thing.

Her heart was in his mouth, his heart held tightly in her palm.

And as it was fearsome cold, she thought it best to climb inside his clothes.

It was then he asked her to explain herself.

I am coal-dark and earth-dirty smudged.

She declared she was feeling coalish, about to burn up, yes she was warming to him, about to ignite off of him and as such she knew then, at that moment it was ashes to ashes, dust to dust.

And he entered her to affirm her existence
and she entered him to lose herself
That by God is the truth

And instinctively she knew, he was and always would be her very own projector/protector/perfector and she would measure beauty against him ever more.

He asked her,
'What do you want from me?'
and she answered,
'Please don't misunderstand me.'

Too much is misunderstood, too many nuances fall by the wayside.

And she spelt it out to make it clear.

SPILT MILK

I love you I love you I love you I love you I love you I love you I love I love you I love you love you I love you
I love you I love you I love you I love you I love I love you I love you I love you I love you I love you I love
you I love you I love you I love I love you I love you I love you I love you I love you I love you I love you I
love you I love I love you I love you I love you I love you I love you I love you I love you I love you I love I
love you I love you I love you I love you I love you I love you I love you I love you I love I love you I love you
I love you I love you I love you I love you I love you I love you I love I love you I love you I love you love
you I love you I love you I love you I love you I love you I love I love you I love you I love you I love you
I love you I love you I love you I love you I love you I love I love you I love you I love you I love you I
love you I love you I love you I love you I love you I love I love you I love you I love you love you
I love you I love you I love you I love you I love you I love I love you I love you love you
love you I love you I love you I love you I love you love you I love you I love
you I love you I love you I love you love you I love you I love you I love
you I love you I love you I love I love you I love you love you I love you
I love you I love you I love you I love you I love I love you I love you I
love you I love you I love you I love you I love you I love you I love I love
you I love you I love you I love you I love you I love you I love you I love
you I love I love you I love you love you I love you I love you I love you
love you I love you I love you I love you I love I love you I love you I love
you I love you I love you I love you I love you I love you I love you I love I
love you I love you love you I love you I love you I love you I love you I love
you I love you I love I love you I love you I love you I love you I love you I
love you I love you I love you I love you I love I love you I love you I love
you I love you I love you I love you I love you I love you I love you I love you
I love I love you I love you love you I love you I love you I love you I love
you I love you I love you I love you I love you I love you I love you I
love I love you I love you I love you I love you I love you I love you I
love you I love you I love you I love I love you I love you I love you
love you I love you I love you I love you I love you I love you I love you
love you I love you I love you I love you I love I love
you I love you I love you I love you I love you I love
you I love you I love you I love you I love you I love
you I love you I love you I love you I love you I love

135

*

NOURISHED on dreams Manfredi wakes beside her.

Rousing slowly, each limb gently shaking the sleep from him. He is silent and in silence he rises to sit up in bed and collect his thoughts for the day, staring straight ahead past the half-shuttered window out to the lake below.

He turns to look at her as she lies horizontal, eyes open and he motions it is time to get up. He pulls the covers from off him and slips his feet into wasting slippers. Similar to the slippers his father used to wear, tartan cloth and worn. Morning naked but for those slippers. He is tall, upright, a long back, lightly tanned skin, drawn taut over his body. She has traced thoughts on that back and written reams in fingerprints.

He stands by the window and gently rubs the back of his neck, then fingers entwined, forces his elbows back, to stretch upward, accompanied by an opening yawn. The coldness of the morning eases over him, goosebumps on his skin. He walks into the bathroom, the door is left wide as he pisses silently and flushes. The faucet runs short and he returns to the bedroom to choose what he will wear, soft clothes of pure textile and he lays them gently at the bottom of the bed.

He looks over at her, as she reaches her hand towards his, the tips of their fingers touching and he says it is time to get up, as still she lies on. He goes back to the bathroom and she can hear the shower water gurgling into action and follows him to sit on the toilet and pee, watching as he washes himself, half listening to her blather on about her dreams. Lathering the soap in his palms, his sharp definition blurs through frosted glass. He washes his face and neck then moves his hands slowly down over his body. He turns the faucet to cold and a sharp morning shock, grabs a towel from the rack and brushes himself dry, back to front, head to toe.

He does this every morning and every morning she watches him.

Dear Mom,

Where to begin?? Where to begin??

I suspect where I left off, jumbo-jetting it to fulfil some dream or other, not even sure now it was my own, but I came anyhow to wander reckless and such false sightings to lose my head over.

Those other escapades . . . Nothing. I swear they were nothing but minor occurrences and in recollection served no other purpose than mere amusement. Mother, to amuse oneself is rather ineffectual. It is a sadly placid emotion, if you can even stretch it to an emotion, and in my condition serving no purpose – where was I?

Lost? Most definitely or maybe just passing through a life that happened to belong to me, at best dithering but at last, eventually Mama, I have struck a balance and, empty, allow myself to replenish.

I suspect and don't think I am being over-gracious but perhaps some of your love germinated within, for there must have been some sort of symptom, a tiny trace apparent and as with that smothered other love which expired so abysmally in the distant past, of which you yourself witnessed, so as with then, I can once more with an incoherent amount of logic blame you. (What are mothers for?) So I blame you and thank you. I thank you and again thank you.

See Mama, he has led me astray and taken me to

a place more beautiful than I have ever imagined. A small plot to unfold upon by a lakeside shore. It is remote and secluded but it is love nonetheless, there is a reminiscence of innocence and purity evident on the out breath, the haw and snowed-over soft, clear skies, I feel like I am home and I'm finding it hard to retain myself.

See it was here, in this icy wilderness, I tripped up, slipped up and lay beneath him, my heart stopping. Stopping short of life and so stretching his humanity over me, he deigned it his moral duty to reawaken my senses . . . and it was not long before I found his tongue lapping, as the heavens the horizon, mine and my lips eased open, to be cradle rocked. Kisses passing back and forth, round and again and once more, repeating ourselves, eagerly, earnestly, like a mischievous truth, as brittle as a flame . . . but even saying so, is, I admit, a fabrication, for it was I who tripped him up.

Indeed before he had reached the ground, I had him in my arms and was pressing my mouth to his, pouring myself upon him, until I felt some sort of return comfort. No matter, for surely the flame supersedes the striking of the match?

Ah, that such a transgression transpired can only be due to this fulsome wonderful disease of love-seekness. I'm certain I already wrote to you about it, this peculiar ailment, making me long for a life of much sickness. I wonder if I have transmitted it, or if he too is an afflicted soul? I know not nor care, as with such things, the wind carries away a thousand caressing fears, leaving me safe to exist, moment by moment, and how I exist – presently, ever in and blinkered from a fatalistic future.

See, seen, foreseen in dreams I told you of. Oh how fortunate hindsight is an afterthought, how wonderful the future cannot impede on the present.

It is the darkest of nights and blind I spy a heaven full of captured kisses. There are some of mine amongst them, for sure, they are shining down upon me.

As always and forever yours,

Murrey

HE counts his lucky stars, then curses the reality that will inevitably intervene.

She holds his hand at every opportunity, sings out of key and tuneless, steals his winter socks as her feet flip-flap in three sizes too big. She made a snow throne and crowned him in flakes, anointing him with kisses. He chops wood so she may light it, cooks so she can fill him with energy, takes long walks with her so that he feels at home, scaring himself with the feelings he has for her.

It is not enough that each night they lay together, beside-inside one another, reaching a point where he feels most female, where she feels most male.

She mumbles in her sleep, sometimes shouting out words of geometry, of circles and squares, calling out, where are you and he answers, right here and places her hand on his heart and the days race on.

Kookie, quirky, knock kneed, nails bitten, beautiful, fragile, fragrant, button ass, sweet belly, hip dip, crooked toes, suede skin and when lying beside her, she tells him stories, impossible tales. Long-tongued, twisting it all the way over, playful pupils and forces them into opposite corners, all the better to see him, she says. He starts a sentence, she finishes it. His mouth widens, she embraces it. His arm rises and she creeps beneath. His eyes open and she is there for him, dismantling him, curious and questioning, and he tells her about his childhood, the kids at school, how they'd pick on him, the class nerd with his red hair and glasses, the one who never got the joke, she laughed and said she was the joke, of awkwardly drifting through adolescence, those long summers of boredom, getting into trouble with Theo, his best friend, hitching round Canada, playing bass in a band, the night Theo had died in a car crash when he'd been there with him. His body mangled and they'd had to cut Theo from out of the car, of coming to Chicago, being hurt by his girlfriend, his father's death and how it affected him and she seemed to understand.

He told her he was in love with her.

She said, 'Love has a lot to answer for.'

I WROTE to my mother, told her my heart was besieged and walls lowered, I had surrendered to him.

We'd been living the simple life and in such isolation it was easy to fall in step with one another. Snowed under, my only wish being we could hibernate and every morning answered true. I recall it as a time I believed in the spiritual, for a fresh fall of white would lie untouched exactly as it had the day before, dressing the landscape in its unearthly silence. Then one morning we woke to find the temperature rising, revealing the beginning of a godawful mess, the driveway up to the house was slush and our snow angels all distorted, resembled cripples.

It was time to move on.

*

The first time I ran away from home, I must have been about five. My faithful bear my sole companion. A pale blue, handknitted affair, with button eyes well sucked upon, the filling, old nylon tights laddered and torn, was grabbed, stuffed into my brown leather, two-buckled satchel, along with a white nightdress Aunt Dora had sent to me from England. Seeking solace from the night sky, twinkle twinkle little star and I wished upon one.

On that occasion, I had it all planned out, I slammed the kitchen door. She was screeching at him, at the end of her tether, infuriated and he sat there taking it all in. Force-fed on anger and docile, the sitting room door locked, so he couldn't slump away and pretend it wasn't happening. Oughtn't he face up to his responsibilities and she deriding him like a piece of dirt, to be swept under the carpet. Her anger spilling over, seeping out under the crack of the door and I'd had enough, so off I took.

Out through the yard and down off into the lane and I reckoned I'd get myself a job in the shop around the corner. Doolin's Newsagent, cause Mr Doolin was always saying how pretty I was, 'Isn't she a fine one you have there missus,' and sometimes he'd give me a coloured Fox's glacier sweet and my mother one too, but only when Mrs Doolin wasn't about.

I bounded down the lane, within sight of the corner shop and already having doubts. It occurred I may have to wait till only Mr Doolin was in the shop, cause Mrs D, a right arse, was sure to send me straight home, not having any time for my nonsense.

'If it's nonsense you're after girl, you've come to the wrong place,' and I'd only been asking her why certain things were the way they were. I would have loved a bit of nonsense and Mr Doolin didn't mind a jot that I was at him all the time, following him up and down the one aisle they had, stacked with household goods and dry foodstuffs. Toilet rolls beside golden syrup beside tins of shoe polish and me asking why for the hundredth time and him answering, 'Like I said before Murrey, that's the way it is.' But why?

'If she says that one more time I'll . . . and where in God's name is her mother? Working is she? Aren't we all and can't her father look after her.' I told Mrs Doolin my dad was cleaning his bicycle.

'Mrs Doolin have a heart, I've just popped in to get him the paper and got waylaid.'

She snorted in response, 'Why aren't you out playing with the others?' There was a question, another unanswered 'why'. Why exactly? Because it's shocking how cruel children can be, saying I was contaminated, when it wasn't like that at all. Tall tales of the Great Depression, a gawdawful time, we didn't have two cents to rub together.

So I told them in sign language, clenched fists raining down on them and the teacher came waddling over, 'I'm not sure I like your behaviour,' and I was made fall in line.

The colour-coded line-up of the primary school. Yellow the weakest of the lot, baby infants, infants, numbers and letters and a stream of 'c's like a small sea of waves, scrawled in HB pencil. Had a mind to march right up and contaminate them. That would give them a shock. Well have you ever? and besides, Mr Doolin didn't mind having the likes of me hanging out of him and then my mother would arrive back from work, all of a fluster, having been home and not finding me there.

My father was meant to have been keeping an eye on me. Could he not even do that.

'Not a problem Mrs Pog, sure she's grand company.'

Mr Doolin gave me a snowball covered in chocolate with desiccated coconut and white sugar snow in the centre.

Outside fogging up Doolin's window with my runaway breath, full of notices, advertisements, bus N'eirrann timetables, Lyon's Family Tea, Mind the Step, No Dogs Allowed. The shutter's down, they must have shut up and gone for their supper, the light above the shop flickering and the curtains drawn.

'Questions, questions, you're a right nosy-parker Miss Murrey Pogue,' says Mrs Doolin, after me asking where her eyebrows had gone to. Had they fallen off or what? Cause she used a black pencil over her eye and I wondered whether it would smudge, if I licked my finger and rubbed. Oi, her hand squeezing my arm hard, 'Run along home, I don't have time to play.' Bejaysus, but I got the distinct feeling she really didn't like me.

My satchel slipped over my shoulders, I'd had enough.

Dad used to spend the whole day polishing his bike, cleaning every spoke, yet wouldn't ride the blasted thing. Where was the sense in that, I ask you.

I lost my nerve, what if I couldn't get a job? It was getting frighteningly dark. I'd come back tomorrow morning, when Mr Doolin was on his own. Sure he'd said to me, 'You'll make a grand shop assistant one day.' My mother was pulling up my socks for me, though I could do it myself, feeling swamped in the school gabardine that had had to be bought three sizes too big.

We didn't have money to burn, don't you know.

About turn, all my high hopes of 'I'll show you' diminished. What was I going to show them anyway and my head hung low. If it wasn't so spooky and black I could camp out in the park, even though I'd never been that far on my own.

Wondering how much trouble I was in, the feeling of defeat dragged at my heels, back down the lane, back home. First, second, third door, having stooped down to clutch at a handful of pebbles and toss them willy-nilly, like parts of myself, as far away as possible. Hurling those pebbles against the yard door, not a light on in the house and it must have been late, later than I'd imagined. Clanging pebbles against the evergreen peeling paint, revealing the old coat of dark red beneath. Then the door opened. My father answered my call.

'What are you up to?'

'What does it look like?'

'Running away?'

I nodded.

'You didn't get very far,' he pointed out the obvious.

'I'll try again tomorrow and the next day and the next day and the . . .'

He said it's best to be prepared, reckoned I'd have to wait a fair few years and then away with me. He pointed up to the starry sky,

'Where were you headed?'

'To America.'

'Like myself.'

'Is that why you're cleaning the bike all the time?'

'It is, so it is,' he chortled in resigned agreement and then turned his attention back to the metal contraption.

Manfredi and I were packing up, heading back to

Chicago. Dylan playing on the car radio as Manfredi loaded up the boot. My head flooded with disjointed memories, unsure of what, exactly, was what, though I'd always count Mr Doolin as one of my friends. He died a few years later, of a broken heart or a coronary attack, I can't be sure. Mrs Doolin moved out of the area and the corner shop was taken on by another couple with seven kids, they were always getting in trouble. They smelt of it.

There was a strange smell, her perfume hit me in the face and she must have gone to all sorts of trouble to trace me here.

That was my first thought.

Understand this, I'd received a letter from my mother.

Suddenly it all began to fall into place. My mother and the blasted magpie. She must have been behind it the whole time. It was her pigeon in disguise, so obvious looking back on it and it made perfect sense.

Followed by an emblem of sorrow all these years, well nothing's ever black and white.

The musky smell of sufferance, of staid stagnant home.

She probably sprayed the paper, enhancing the guilt factor. Mothers, and they are always overstepping the mark, to then hit the point exactly. This was supposed to be a one-way communication, couldn't she have left things as they were. It would just get more complicated, her interfering, throwing up a host of unanswered questions. Why and why, and . . . why it had to happen in the first place.

Mrs Calder and I'm sure what she did is a federal offence.

Mrs Calder, or to put it more aptly, the Revenge of the Storekeepers.

We'd pulled up outside Johann Calder's Grocery and Haberdashery to fill up on necessities, gas and groceries. A weekly occurrence since our arrival up at the lake.

Inside, Mrs Calder, a sprightly seventy-five year old, sat knitting a jumper for one of her great grand-children, the TV blaring kept her company and she was immersed in a rerun of *The Brady Bunch*. On each visit I had been introduced to a different member of the family. Our presence brought her to her slippered feet and she laid the beginnings of a pink cardigan to one side, then lowered the volume of the set. Pressing her palms down on her patterned apron, she wiped flat the creases in preparation for a sale and bid us both a good afternoon. Manfredi had warned me about her drilling questions, name?, where did I come from?, how long was I staying?, did I happen to know any members of the Irish branch of the Calder family?, how old was I?

Murrey, Ireland, pass, no not that I recall, I stopped counting at seven. Phew and not so bad in comparison with Mrs Doolin, with her, who did I think I was? Someone. Where did I think I was going? Somewhere. Would you ever act your age? All of five and three quarters at the time and I thought I was.

Mrs Calder turned her attention to Manfredi, giving me time to recover. Had I said too much, had I let anything slip. Her concern understandable having known Manfredi a long while. Practically asking if I was good enough, rotten through and through, and I left them chatting to pace through the store, doubting my own integrity.

146

Caught fragments of concern and sympathy voiced about people in the area I didn't know, issues I'd no interest in, the dwindling community, the misplanting of fir trees at the expense of elms. The conversation close to exhaustion, my basket overbrimming with enough for a week and Manfredi impressing upon Mrs Calder that her family were, as always, more than welcome to visit him in Chicago any time.

'Any time Mrs Calder,' repeating himself, safe in the knowledge she would never come.

And before she forgets, 'A letter came in for your girlfriend,' pointing at me.

How so and again with my questions, 'Are you sure, for me?'

Disbelief and concerned she had misplaced it.

Delivered to the Calder post office-cum-general store, earlier that very morning, just waiting to be claimed and wasn't it perfect timing you stopping by this afternoon.

Was it?

'But of course,' spluttered Mrs Calder, suddenly all a fluster and she began rummaging through the drawers looking for the letter.

The possibility perplexing me.

'Do you know who it's from?'

Carefully, slowly, Mrs Calder fingered through a small batch of letters. Why was she taking so long, why? why?

'Your mother I think,' she carried on pushing the batch aside, 'Now I wonder where I've gone and left it.'

She shuffled off into the back part of the shop. 'I never read it mind, see there's a return address on it.' She held up a crumpled rose-coloured envelope and handed the letter over.

I was in a state of percussion, my heart pounding, doing the utmost not to make it obvious, as a chill spread through my spine like liquid ice. I didn't snatch it but waited for Mrs Calder to hand the letter over. A meagre thanks offered, as I extracted myself from two pairs of prying eyes and went out to the parking lot, to the privacy of the car.

Just now when everything had hit an even keel to haunt me with her presence. She wrote:

My dear dear Murrey,

I wasn't certain you'd ever forgive me. I'm still not sure you have but thank you for your last letter. How happy I am and how wonderful for you to have at last found your feet, dare I say it, entrenched in love. I sincerely hope this man is deserving of my daughter.

I am trying desperately hard not be over-emotional so if the tone of this letter strikes you as being odd, there is of course good reason. For so long Murrey I cherished all those cards you sent over the years, but try to imagine how much I have wanted to write back and sending off letters to post-marks in big cities like New York or LA just didn't stand a chance and all were returned to sender. How fortunate to find a return address stamped on the back of the envelope (*Seasonal greetings from Johann Calders, for all your holiday needs, etc.*), so please don't be angry, I really couldn't prevent myself from replying in the hope you may receive this letter.

A lot has happened since your departure, almost five years and now as I sit here writing I am suddenly left wordless and really don't know where to begin.

The present will have to suffice, as everything else seems to be wildly out of context and must wait until the time when, God blessing, we may be with one another again.

I am well and really can't complain, though my hair is now grey and my middle more portly. Recently I bumped into a woman called Margaret. We used to work together a long time ago before she went to live in the States. It must be twenty years since I've seen her and it was by chance I ran into her on my way to the butchers, of course both of us declared, 'You haven't changed a bit!!' (if only) and for the last while we have been, as you would probably say yourself, 'hanging out together'. I belong to various committees, probably dreadfully dull in comparison to your life and lately took up square-dancing, which is all the rage here. On Wednesdays, Margaret and I go off to the local church hall. I have to say it has been marvellous to dance again. I hadn't danced for such a while, since your dad and I used to empty the hall with our rock and rolling.

Murrey I am so glad you are happy at last. Please keep writing.

Many, many kisses
Much love
Mum

PS. May this love leave you breathless and prevent you from ever running again.
PPS. Please send a picture if you get a moment.
PPPS. I was only ever trying to do my best, I hope you believe this. I know I made mistakes and I'm sorry.

*

SUDDENLY silenced and ashen-faced, Murrey asked Manfredi to meet her in the car park.

'I hope it's not bad news Manfredi,' Mrs Calder whispered, whittling on as she rang up the groceries on an old-fashioned till.

Manfredi paid her, then carried the bags out to the car. Murrey stood leant up against the edge, biting at the skin on the side of her left thumb.

'Good news?' he asked, referring to the letter.

'Mmm,' she replied, obviously not wishing to elaborate.

Slamming the boot of the car down.

'You want to talk about it?'

'Nah,' she half groaned, chewing on a nail.

Silent the whole journey back and then she had wandered off. Alone, down to the frozen shoreline, to catch the last embers of light in her stride. She borrowed one of his jackets, draped it across her shoulders, her dark hair drawn back off her face and buried beneath a woollen hat. She left Manfredi to unload the groceries, walking away from him, plucking at evergreens to slowly shred them, then bend forward to pick up a pine cone and roll it in her hands before discarding it. She had a habit of humming softly, any tune or many, merging, one into another and oftentimes she would sing aloud, unaware of scavenged notes on a tailwind floating back to him, but the stillness of that afternoon carried only a sullen silence. From Manfredi's point of view, he could just make out her movements, she sat hunched over, cross-legged on the old rickety mooring, shifting round to look back at the house half hidden by trees and shrubbery, unable to glimpse him watching.

He waited for her to return, observed her backtrack, up towards the house, each step closer-further and she removed his jacket from across her shoulders and hung it on the peg inside the door.

'It's freezing,' she remarked, 'You hungry?'

Few words passed between them as they went about the daily chores, he to build a fire and she to the kitchen and it was there he found her, chopping onions, her face streaked red.

'You okay Murrey?'

She turned towards him.

'Sure. It's the onions.' He approached but she shrugged him off.

'You going to tell me what's up?'

'There's nothing to say.'

The fire blazing and the evening spent watching flames dance, till the last of the ashes flickered to extinguish their red glow. She sat as usual, curled up on the sofa reading and he on the floor below. Again he asked what the matter was, in answer she merely smiled awkwardly. He saw her eyes cloud over, her forehead crease. Rubbing her hands over her face, she forced a yawn then excused herself, claiming to have a headache.

He found the letter. Later that evening and restless, Manfredi began to tidy the room.

Her book, balanced on the arm of the chair, fell and tumbled out its contents. The letter from abroad and turning the envelope over in his hand, Manfredi deliberated whether he should or shouldn't read it. Return to sender, clearly marked on old-fashioned paper, obviously part of a writing set. A sprig of posies printed in one corner and the handwriting slanted and small.

Focused on the address, should he, or shouldn't he read it? He placed the letter down, picked it up, sighed before finally slipping it back in the pages of the book. To trespass on a secret that wasn't his, yet aware of how she seemed to be curling back into herself.

He crept into bed, beneath the covers. Murrey lay rolled away from him asleep and as he bent over to kiss her lightly he felt her cheeks moistened, to taste the salt of her tears.

Lying alongside one another, it was a while before he sensed her stir from the bed, to footstep falter across the floorboards aching. She shuffled into his slippers, then creaked down the stairs. He let her go, sighing in the dim glow of a morning waking.

'Murrey,' he cried, 'come on it's time to go.'

Manfredi had checked and double-checked everything was off, sockets, faucets, the grate cleared, house locked and car loaded up. He stood on the porch, rubbing together his frozen fingers. Murrey within his view, shifted from foot to foot, down at the jetty by the lake.

The time had passed by too quickly, thirty days spent and he felt short-changed.

Murrey and himself absorbed in one another, so that nothing else existed. The ground dissolved from beneath his feet and she had caught him. Giddy on her and every moment memorable and she had set to, capturing them on an old Kodak Instamatic. Ordering Manfredi to stand motionless, this way or that, posturing at her request so she could snap. Hours flashed by, the timer ticking and she would jump into frame to join him.

The taste of her lingered on his tongue and an image of the small of her back played at the back of his mind. Rewind to the night before, to where he was standing.

On the porch, music from the front room spilling outside, notes caught in cold breath. She sat wrapped in the duvet, in order she claimed to keep his smell about her. Her comfort blanket, the covers drawn up close around her and she immersed in counterfeit fiction. Warm beside one another, Manfredi brushed back loose strands of hair from off her face, to see her clearly, his reaction impulsive and he reached forward, offering his lips, to feel her teeth imprint upon them.

'But seriously,' she said and out of nowhere. 'If I lose you, will you follow?'

He didn't understand.

She repeated herself. Manfredi denied the possibility.

'I'm not about to lose you.'

'Hypothetically, if one day you were to.'

'Murrey I'm not going to lose you.'

'I just want an answer, would you seek me out?'

'What do you want me to say?'

'The truth.'

'Why can't you ever be straightforward?'

Her logic defied him, a sadness she carried within, those unfathomable secrets he had yet to uncover.

Manfredi cupped his hands and shouted once again, 'Murrey we should leave now, before it gets dark.'

I LEFT Manfredi to pack up while I dirt-tracked it down to the lakeside shore one last time to tease out my worries. See I was cautious about meeting Manfredi's friends and our bubble bursting, making another mess in my head. After all we had begun on such a good note, full throttle almost strangling. How long before one of us would run out of breath?

To be always looking ahead, a habit of mine acquired on my travels, sometimes wished my neck would snap so I could loll.

Oh to loll, wishing to call time to a halt, as I tarried down by the lake, hands gloved, hat pulled down over my head. I was skimming pebbles off the iced water.

No ripples rendered and I took it as a good sign, everything would be okay.

If I kept repeating it, then everything would be okay.

The car loaded and ready to go, Manfredi was calling out to me. I climbed the small slope, each step bigger on the incline.

We were bound for Chicago.

Mile after mile dissolved beneath us, creating distance. Spurts of conversation, a crackling radio, the inside warm and a stock of crisps and sweets, bought specially for the journey. Car games of yes and no, do you love me, I do, are you sure? I am, marry me, I might, say yes, I will not, say yes, you can't make me, say no, and destroy everything we have together?, give me a definitive answer, I will, a yes or a no. Impossible, then you'd win the game, you're too good at this, well I've been on the road a long time.

Manfredi yawned. What next, I-spy with my little eye? There were absolutely no red, blue or green cars to count. There were no cars on the road. Nothing but sky, tarmac and forest. Time for a sweet break and bored, I asked Manfredi if he wanted some chocolate.

'Come on,' he insisted, 'You're meant to amuse me, keep me awake at the wheel. I-spy or a story.'

Maybe a bit of both, though closer to the truth and I admitted to Manfredi to being a veteran spy.

A long time ago, in a faraway land, I was a keyhole spy. Viewing the world from behind closed doors, with a particular perspective. I'd witnessed a host of scenes played out by knees. All sorts: tight, sagging, old, young, scuffed, scabbed, scarred, false limbed, nude, hairy, clothed, shattered, knocking.

Fat pudgy knees like Mrs Bunion's.

Now there's a story.

She wore dark natural tan popsocks, stopping just below the knee of short plump legs that met with a load of straggling veins, like some aerial cartography. At the end of a day her socks would roll in a particular curling manner down to her calf, leaving an elastic imprint. Mrs Bunion lived a few doors up the road and had taken a certain shine to me.

I called her Bunion the Onion, cause she smelt and her feet were misshapen. She would take her shoes off but not her popsocks, which were always riddled with ladders and it looked like she had two extra toes sprouting on either side of her feet. She would sit rubbing them in the kitchen while my mother prepared the tea. The pair of them gossiping over a boiling kettle and I'd hear them nattering.

My mother moaning on about my father, who had recently lost his job. 'No good to no one. If it wasn't for the little one I'd up and leave.'

Bunion, scratching at her feet, would reprimand my mother, 'You're a fool missus. It's just a phase he's going through, it'll be all right.'

'Out in that blasted shed, day-in day-out. He has me at the end of my tether, he's not going to get anywhere sitting on his backside all day.'

I was listening in, hanging off the door outside, dangling from the knob as only a person my height could, except the handle shifted. My mother must have sensed something cause the knob turned and I lost my balance and collapsed.

'What in God's name . . . ?'

My mother pushed the door open to find me heaped on the heavily patterned red carpet.

'How long have you been there?'

At a time when I had just managed to grasp the difference between the big hand and the little hand, my shoulders raised upward in confused shruggery.

'Ah leave her,' muttered Bunion in my defence.

'Were you listening in?' demanded my mother.

To nod guiltily and be sore slapped on the back of the legs.

'She didn't mean anything, did you little one?'

Bunion grabbed me by the arm and dragged me over to her, less threatening than the glare of my mother.

'And isn't she only the spitting image of her daddy.'

I'd try and stay as far back as I could, avoiding Bunion's earthy aroma and pincer-action fingers but she would wag my cheek from off my face and me holding in my breath, trying to stay at arm's length, the back of my thigh smarting, hearing my mother's voice,

'How many times do I have to tell you, not to be listening in on other people's business?'

'Sure she doesn't understand.' Both cheeks clasped and I agreed with Bunion I'd totally lost the plot and also my balance, as I stepped on her toe or her bunion, not sure which, but my cheeks were automatically released as she squealed in agony and I received another slap, unfortunately on the same thigh. It was time to scarper out the back but not before being made to apologize.

Our backyard, twenty foot by twenty, same as every other in a row of terraced houses. My bedroom window looked out over it, down on to the shed, my father's refuge, where he'd disappear into for days at a time. His black bike leant up against the yard wall. The shed was timber which he'd built himself, demolishing an old outhouse. He would go and smoke there, Players Blue, hammer and nail, banging together pieces of wood to make himself useful.

Beside his bike was a large coal bin always full, another smaller one for logs and a backyard door leading out on to a lane. He'd usually arrive home from work and disappear into the shed while I played.

I'd chalk numbers on to outlined squares in tower patterns no architect would approve of, for it was lateral to jump from square one to square ten, in nine easy hops etched in yellow, blue or pink chalk.

My mother would call us in for tea, sticking her head out the kitchen window, to holler till we two left what we were at and came in. Hands washed and sat at the plain wood table while my mother balanced pots and pans and dished out whatever we had coming.

'You had it coming to you Tom, so don't expect any sympathy from me.'

He was a quiet man, a private man and would never answer back, remaining silent, chewing carefully over every morsel. Tea was always silent in our house, heavy sticking in my throat. I knew nothing then, of anything but that that was how it was. Dad worked at the general post office until the strike and when the strike ended he never went back.

Last in first out, that's the way it goes.

To scarper out to the yard. I didn't know he was in the shed, the bike wasn't perched up against the wall, where it usually was. I assumed he was off on one of his wanders.

I had run out into the yard, my socks fallen down around my ankles, thigh tingling and my chalk stick sodden, for it must have been raining and I ran towards the shed in my haste to escape my mother and Bunion. I guess I was looking for a place of refuge and I burst through the door and my father was sitting inside.

I hadn't expected him to be there.

Usually I'd hear the hammer and tong, the chaffing or sawing.

I hadn't expected to see him, sitting there immobile.

'She's leaving you,' I said, 'You're bloody useless.'

He motioned me to close the door.

Didn't my mother have to sell his bike to pay the feckin bills. She had had to go out and get a job. They had danced their last and he would never be going to America.

'Bill Haley?' she'd say. 'Sure he's a one-eyed kiss-curled infatuation and anyhow what would you want to be going to America for now?'

But he would forever go on about it.

'America, you're worse than the child,' and he would look at me.

My father started having terrible headaches, they'd last a whole week. He'd come in to the house to eat, then disappear out to his shed again. I imagined he must have been building a rocket ship to take us to America.

I hardly saw him anymore and if I did I always seemed to be under his feet. Fancy footwork the two of us hopscotching one another.

Then he left just like that.
Just like that.

'You okay Murrey?'
Manfredi leant forward.
'Huh?'
'You were about to say something, about Bunion, a neighbour.'
'Oh yeah.' I yawned and apologized, whatever it was had gone clear out of my head.
'You sure you're okay?'
'Yes.'
'Ha, made you say yes, I win,' Manfredi gloated.

The game almost up.
Then highway driving and I was lost in dark dreams on a homeward journey, my sights fixed upon the descending dusk, on the tail-end of that one last look.

Sidereal Time

She left him
  Just like that.

Manfredi woke up alone, it was the beginning of summer. Thunderstorms rolled in from the lake as he edged over in the bed to the empty space beside him. Burrowing his head beneath the pillow, desperate to find a trace of Murrey's scent, his whole body ached, each limb uncomfortable in its socket, heavy with the feeling of nausea. It weighed him down, the only thing he could depend on, to keep him steady.

In hindsight, Manfredi should have seen it coming, or prevented what occurred from happening. When he reflected back in the white glow of clarity, this is what he thought. He wanted to hate her, to flip sides, urged time to fast-forward, to when he could pity her. Then he'd know everything would be all right.

She left in a sudden gale, ran from him with excuses, she was drenched in excuses.

It didn't make sense to him, hard to pin down what exactly had happened.

What exactly had happened?

Step by step he mulled over the past six months as if teasing a yarn.

*

She had moved into his apartment straight off. Manfredi had ignored Sol's premonitions that 'in a couple of weeks, you won't know the place'. Of course Sol was proved wrong. Having brought nothing with her but one large cumbersome suitcase, the flat remained unchanged, except for the paintings in the main room. She had taken them down, replacing the empty space with a montage of photos taken from up at the lake and a cheap nasty calendar. In retrospect Manfredi realized this was probably the first sign, the very fact she had never really made it her home.

On the day of their return, Sol was waiting at the apartment to welcome them back. In their absence he'd been keeping an eye on it. Manfredi pushed open the door to find Sol draped in an apron, taking a home-made cheesecake from out of the oven.

'Hey Manfredi, welcome back,' and before Manfredi could get a word in, Sol disclosed the news of his ex fiancée's imminent marriage.

'I was right about Charlie all along. Charles Sugarman, a lousy eye doctor. Believe me, he's welcome to her,' vented Sol, the words spluttering out in defiance. Fredi, I'm a new man.' He patted his stomach, 'You think I lost any weight?'

'Yeah . . . the apartment . . . looks . . .' Overwhelmed, Manfredi placed down his bags, trying to remember the chaotic mess he'd left the place in.

'Tidy? I hope you don't mind, but I got in professional cleaners, a welcome home, Christmas present.'

'It's great Sol,' Manfredi gasped, trying to figure if Sol had undergone a lobotomy.

'A new year's resolution,' Sol explained in answer to

Manfredi's expression. 'Don't worry, it's sure to wear thin.'

The place was heavy with the smell of good cooking, as the cheesecake steamed gently on a wire cooling rack.

'So where's Murrey?'

She was on her way up, accompanying the final load in the elevator.

'You two have a good time? You look like you had a good time.'

Just then Murrey pushed through the door as if she'd done it a million times before.

'I guess you must be Sol.' She introduced herself. 'Manfredi's told me stacks about you.'

'Hey,' and Sol balked, 'Have we met before?'

Her head shook a negative response, 'I don't think so.'

'I'm sure we've met before, your voice it seems familiar.'

'Are you coming on to me?' she giggled and Sol blushed.

Sol pulled a bottle of celebratory champagne from the refrigerator, clenched it between his knees and yanking free the cork, three glasses were raised and they toasted to whatever lay before them. Champagne and cheesecake and it melted on their tongues and greedy they forked it in large dollops.

Of course she was full of praise for the chef, quite overdoing it, Manfredi thought, while Sol lapped it up.

'Murrey, I like you already,' he schmoozed, digging his fork into the last gluttonous mouthful.

You could compare it, the sense that is, to searching for a silver lining, rather than a clear blue sky. The supposition that happiness is an emotion on loan, pink as sand in an upturned egg-timer, fast flowing towards gravity.

Fact was, since my arrival in the land of Mickey Mouse, I had merely skimmed the surface, on the lookout for what was round the corner and living like some heightened tourist. But at last I felt or was beginning to feel the corner had been turned. I spent time exploring the city, from merely existing to living and there seemed for once real possibilities. Dipping my toes in square two, I eased into Manfredi's life. I liked his life.

I would just sit taking him in, so comfortable in his closeness. This transmutater, celluloid buffer, stacks of evenings, afternoons spent projecting ourselves, one on to another. He'd asked me to define myself, I told him I was a good-for-nothing, no-hoper, dreamer who had lost her way in the land of nod and was just about to wake up.

He didn't mind, said I had youth on my side and reckoned I had time enough to develop a sense of perspective.

See, he seemed to make sense out of me.

And I liked that.

Upon our return, I gave up working at Clear Glazers. I didn't have a choice and consoled myself with the thought that those types of jobs are two-a-penny. To prove the point, I got shiftwork cleaning offices.

It was a muggy day, overcast grey and, on reflection, first doubts unearthed as winter melted into spring. I woke late, the night's imprint upon me, creased with sleep. Misshapen by a heavy slumber or violent dream,

I found myself alone in the flat. Manfredi had already left for the studio and I rang work, explaining I'd suffered a severe bout of Dreamer's Disease and would have to take the day off.

'Are you for real?' asked my boss.

'Hey I swear to you. It's an established ailment, inner cranial turbulence caused by the overworking of an optic nerve. Dr Dreamer is up there with the likes of Dre, Watson, Who, Dolittle and Wassup. Frankly I've too much to lose and you know how much I depend on my job.'

I crossed my fingers, crossed my legs.

'Girl you're full of shit.'

'Thanks. Thanks a lot boss.'

Okay, so what if I had been late for work, like every shift, ever. In this day and age you've got to be flexible.

'And another thing,' he says to me, 'You're fired.'

'Now hold on a minute,' but he wouldn't listen and said it had been due to my ineptness that his company had lost their biggest client. The shame of it, but really how the hell was I to decipher which papers to shred?

Two piles of paper had been left on the MD's desk. One headed 'Scrap', the other, 'AGM Minutes, Private and Confidential, Do Not Remove'.

'You know boss, the problem with this country is? It's obsessed by time. So I chucked a few minutes. Big Deal.'

Cast in gloom, I sighed heavily, another sacking. Not that I'd really wanted the job, but it meant having to mill that circle again. Then I realized Debra had mentioned they were short-staffed at Al's. I called Manfredi and asked if he thought it a good idea. Apparently the best, Debra agreed too, on condition of persistent punctuality. I assured her I lived by the clock. I was to start the following morning. At once I set forth on a mission, to find a perfect American smile and inflection, for 'Have a nice day'.

STARING up at the bedroom ceiling, hands clasped, behind his head, Manfredi was searching for answers, of why Murrey left so suddenly. Recalling seeded doubts, when one evening he had stopped by Al's, on the way home from the studio.

'Can't be that bad,' Debra had remarked, finger snapping Manfredi out of internal deliberations, creasing his forehead in an unflattering way.

'Huh?'

'You look preoccupied, bordering on worried,' she squeezed in alongside of him, a beer bottle in each hand. Then in one continuous movement, she spat some gum into an ashtray, took a pack of all natural American Spirit out of her shirt pocket, flicked it open, flipped one out, caught it in her mouth, lit it, drew in a long breath and finally exhaled a ribbon of smoke.

They sat speechless for a few moments, beside one another.

It had been a good while since Debra and he had spent an evening together.

Manfredi had been feeling out of sorts, an instinctive hunch he had been unable to shake. It bothered him, niggled at the back of his mind, the possibility Murrey may take off or disappear.

At the time he'd put it down to insecurity. He had thought that must be it, as everything between them was going well. Couldn't really get any better. The sole snag had been her vague answers in relation to questions on her past. 'What does it matter?' she'd reply and always managed to avoid specifics, leaving him with imprints. A less than perfect picture of wide brushstrokes.

He told himself he was stupid to press her, her past wasn't so important, this unknown entity he had fallen for and how far he had fallen.

Once, when he'd taken her skating on State St, she had boasted she could cry at the drop of a hat.

'You know like a proper actress,' and he had answered,

'Yeah sure.'

'It's true, I swear.'

'Sure.'

'Cross my heart. It's true.'

She'd just quit her cleaning job and wanted to celebrate.

'I mean how can anyone expect me to work in such conditions?'

He'd asked if she wanted to go ice skating. She answered she'd never skated before.

A pair of fools, slip circling one another and she clung to the bottom of his jacket as he dragged her round, confident enough at the end of an hour to attempt to race him. She lost, tumbled into his arms and dragged him down with her.

'Cheat,' he cried.

'Rubbish, if you were any good, you would have got away by now.'

So they raced again and again and he won every time.

'I love you,' he'd blared out, swooping down upon her.

'Even though I'm a loser.'

'Even though,' and lifting her up in his arms, he skated with her over to the exit.

They sat unlacing their boots on the bench, and she had made some stupid comment about crying. He hadn't believed her.

'Okay look,' and it was as if she had entered inside of herself, her lower lip quivered and the smallest of tears began to flow down her cheeks.

'Bravo,' he applauded, had taken out his handkerchief and dabbed the corners of her eyes.

'Yeah but sometimes it's hard to stop.' She apologized, tears flowing, her cheeks soon soaked, eyes slightly swelling and she tried to laugh it off, but her nose continued running and she had to put her hand up to her face, to hide its contorting.

He held her tight, till those waves of sadness subsided to ripples and her breathing became easy again.

Tiny black rivers streaked her face like cartoon lashes gone awry.

'Sorry,' she snivelled. 'My mother always said I never knew when to stop. Sorry,' and she squeezed his hand and suggested they go someplace else.

'But I was good hey? Convincing? Sometimes I think I may have missed my vocation.'

He'd clasped his hands either side of her face then bent forward, to kiss her hard on her mouth.

Disbelief, not knowing where the sadness came from, thinking she had summoned it up there and then, but had she? He wasn't sure, uncertain of everything. Unable to pin the feeling down and that was precisely it.

In Al's, with Debra, Manfredi reached forward and

took a slug from the beer bottle placed in front of him, ready to shrug off his preoccupations.

'How come you smoking American Spirit?'

'I'm on a health kick.' Debra belched loudly. The last of the customers long gone, the door sign had rotated to *closed* shortly after Manfredi's arrival.

Rubbing her eyes, Debra yawned.

'So what's up Manfredi?'

'It's Murrey.'

'Figures. Let me see,' Debra surmised, 'You can't put your finger on it, but something isn't quite right.'

'Yeah. How'd'you guess?'

'It's that particular look on your face.'

'Which look?'

'Kinda similar to the one you used when you'd had enough of Kelly, and what was her name Trica, and before that Sara.'

It wasn't like that at all. Debra had lost him, was on the wrong track all together.

'Jesus Debra, you're way off the mark.'

'Sorry Manfredi, it's just . . .'

Sighing deeply, their roles reversed and Debra's protective aloofness disintegrated. Her eyelids lowered, her cigarette stubbed out and right hand placed over her mouth.

'Sorry it's just . . . everything,' she groaned, before splurging out a stream of vitriol she'd been hoping to spew at Tomas.

'I found out he's seeing someone else. This is besides me and his wife.'

'How do you know?'

'Because I know.' She went to get a couple more beers and began filling Manfredi in on the most miserable holiday season. She understood most of it would

169

be spent with his family but on the one night they'd arranged to see each other Tomas cancelled. He called an hour before he was meant to pick her up, to say he wouldn't be able to make it. Explained how his youngest boy had been rushed into accident and emergency. His little finger hung off his hand, having been jarred in a car door.

'No way,' she'd cried, cause she'd heard the story before.

She star 69'd to check the number. He'd called from a bar on the other side of town, nowhere near a hospital.

Another couple of bottles emptied, another couple opened.

Manfredi figured Debra'd be better off alone.

'It's the lying I can't hack. Tell me, why do liars assume simplicity in those they lie to? Not that Tomas had said a word and I guess that's it. If he'd told me, it wouldn't seem such a deal. It's those hidden extras that cause such havoc. Why couldn't he just be straight?'

'Some guys . . . it's a way of life, a warped protection thing. So you going to leave him?'

'Manfredi . . . fuck it, you know, it's kinda lonely.'

His arm stretched across her shoulders, pulling her in close,

'It'll be okay. You'll meet someone else.'

'When?' her voice despondent and choked.

Debra took a serviette from the steel dispenser and blew her nose.

'So what's up with you and Murrey?'

Manfredi did his best to explain. He'd been feeling vulnerable. In matters of love, he'd always held the upper hand.

'Maybe you've met your match.'

How he wished it were so, tinder struck and scared in case it blew up in his face.

'Whatever, it's like having a teenage flashback . . .'

Interrupted by a tapping on the window, they both turned sharply.

'Who the fuck?'

It was Sol, his face pressed up against the darkness of the outside pane. He waved in at them.

Manfredi turned back, 'I guess you should let him in.'

Debra went to open up.

'Hey anyone want a drink?' he cheered, popping his head around the door, his body swiftly in pursuit.

Manfredi declined, it was getting late and he'd told Murrey he'd be home early.

'Debra, what about you?' Sol's gaze turned on Debra.

'No thanks,' she replied.

'Go on, just the one,' coaxed Sol.

Manfredi could tell Sol was attempting to hit on her.

'You know I remember you from the Soul Kitchen.'

'Is that right?'

'Sure you were with that guy in the band. Come to think of it I'm organizing a convention, you reckon he may be interested in playing at it?'

'I wouldn't know,' her abrupt tone translating to Sol as a green light.

'So what about a bite to eat then?' he continued.

Debra raised her brows at Manfredi.

'Is this guy kosher?'

And Sol answered for him.

'The real McCoy.'

*

Outside the café, Manfredi watched as they walked over to Sol's car, then turned on his heels, ready to make his way back to the apartment.

There he found Murrey flicking randomly from one channel to the next. Obviously agitated, she gruffly mumbled something about a postcard on the kitchen bar. The postcard was from Kelly, a fleeting thinking of you in purple ink, with love from the Big Apple and just to let him know she'd be back soon, kiss, kiss.

He threw it to the side, discarding it without a second glance.

'Where have you been?' asked Murrey, her arms folded across her chest. Manfredi plonked himself down in the sofa beside her. She inched away from him, 'So?'

Of course he ought to have said, Kelly? She's an ex-girlfriend and it's no big deal. Instead of which, he shoved the question back towards her. 'That's rich Murrey, I mean where have you been?'

'All over,' she sneered at him.

All over and she left him. That which he had feared the most happened. Tossing and turning alone in his bed Manfredi found a spot, a remnant of her presence, on the edge of the pillow. He took a deep breath and buried his nose in it.

PERHAPS I talked too much or maybe Manfredi just asked too many questions, but every time I answered it was like I was giving the wrong one, even when it was the truth.

I tried telling him. Maybe not the correct way but in the only way I knew how.

Yet he kept on, wanted to know everything. Consider it a type of game. He egged me further. I'm crap at games, I admitted.

I went to kiss him but he pushed me away.

Zebedi was right that time when he threw me out with the words, 'You're not a real player, this has to stop.' I should have listened, instead of crawling back and losing out big time.

Going round in circles and would I ever take heed?

'It's just a game Murrey,' Manfredi argued, rolling the dice, to fall on a six and throw out another blasted question.

A game of truth and there I was losing badly.

Suddenly felt defenceless, like the time when I worked as a pump attendant on that lost highway.

All day, everyday, twenty-four hours, alone in a shack of a gas station and the owner would drop by at various times to pick up his takings. It was a period of great stagnation for the road was long and mostly empty, a couple of vehicles, a few stray bushels and the odd lizard passing by. Nothing much happening until I met Maggie May.

Maggie May had piercing blue eyes and raven-black hair. She swerved to a standstill at the side of the road, wearing dark glasses, a scarf and swigging whiskey from out of a bottle. I swaggered over in my dirty denims, an oil-cloth hanging from the waistband. Obviously drunk, she demanded I fill her up, so I went to get her some coffee.

Her shades pushed up revealed glazed-over eyes and she stumbled out of her car, cigarette in hand, over to a small patch of grass. A spot where drivers let their dogs shit after a long journey.

When I wandered back, she was sat cross-legged, flicking dried pieces of crap across the newly tar-macked stretch of highway the owner was so proud of.

'Ain't it funny how you never see white doggie-do anymore?' she remarked.

'Never noticed,' I replied, handing her the mug and asked where she was headed.

'Wherever the road takes me.'

I fetched an old sweeping brush from the shack and brushed it over the tarmac, clearing it, in case the owner turned up and accused me of not taking proper care of his property.

She looked at me aghast, 'Sweetheart, you some sort of retard?'

I dunno but the tone of her voice just got to me and I felt as if someone had smashed me across the face. Embarrassingly I started to sniff. She threw over a handkerchief.

'I'm sorry,' I said, 'No one's ever called me sweet-heart before.'

Maggie May offered me a ride and the long and short of it was, I joined her on a Midwestern adventure.

Maggie May was fleeing an oppressively humdrum life as a housewife buried to a boring husband. Her routine had remained unchanged for five years which felt like twenty. Her whole life revolved around the TV, sitcoms, soaps and confessional shows, the mall and all-in package holidays to the same place where you could eat and drink as much as you liked. This staid existence served only to make her feel invisible and she wanted adventure, she wanted to see a bit of the world before she gave up colouring her grey hairs black and started dying them blue, wanted to taste a slice of the real thing, rather than view it through the huge TV in the corner of her front room.

Greedy for experiences we went wild, like two kids in a candystore, freaking out on E numbers. Neither of us had had such fun for years. I swear it was like putting all your fears to one side and just going out there and grabbing opportunities. Only difference being that if you're going to play close to the edge, the likelihood is you'll lose your balance and fall.

Clocking miles, we sped toward a drastic evening, beginning earlier in the day when we'd pulled over at a cheap motel. It was fairly crude, no big deal, the sheets worn and smelling of cheap industrial detergent.

We decided to spend the afternoon by the empty pool, drinking and laughing with Alfonso. He was the manager, a seedy, greasy, fly-swatting, shirt sweat-stained geezer. He told us about a dance on later that evening, said if we were up to it, it would be a hoot.

We were and later on we went into town, laughing all the way. It was toe-tapping, foot-hopping, spinning an' a cussin' and we didn't notice time fly and then, after the bar had closed, Alfonso drove us back with a couple of his mates. We didn't smell the danger. Doused in alcohol, they kept passing us bottles of snake-eye or snake-grass or whatever, just to keep us moist. We were shrieking with laughter and then suddenly I felt ill. I could see stars but they weren't the celestial type and I heaved up everything all over me and the smell was something putrid. I curled up and conked out over the bathroom sink, the faucet running on my face. In the other room I could hear them having fun. Not sure how long I'd passed out for, but when I came to Maggie was still howling, only this time not with laughter. I puked up the rest of my drunkenness and let the adrenalin flow through me. Shaking, I knew she was in danger, knew I was next on the agenda. Moving as quietly, as slowly as possible, I closed the door that I'd left slightly ajar and locked it. There was a small shaft above the sink, a most modest form of air-conditioning and I climbed up and miraculously out. I ran to the car. If I could make it to the car I'd be okay. Maggie May kept a rifle in the back and I knew I had to act fast. I grabbed the rifle and shot open the motel room door; the men were taken aback and I gave one a bullet straight between the eyes. Pointed to his brains oozing down the wall, to let the others know I meant business. Maggie was in a bit of a state and I told her to go get in the car and I'd meet her there.

Then I forced Alfonso to tie his friend to the bed, tight as can be and I shot him in the abdomen so that he'd slowly bleed to death. Next I ordered Alfonso to walk the plank, climb the highest diving-board and take a running jump.

The pool was empty of water. See I wanted to impress the point upon him, that when a motel advertises use of a swimming pool, that's exactly what he should have provided. A pool with water. In the sweltering heat people like to swim. I gave him a choice, he could either jump or I'd shoot him off the board. Thing was it was a bluff, I'd run out of cartridges and the goddarn slob asked me to shoot.

Double bluff.

Manfredi interrupted me,

'Murrey will you for godsakes talk to me,' he pleaded, 'Why be so evasive, what are you hiding from, Murrey?'

176

I'd turned up the volume on the TV set, real loud to drown out his questions.

He'd risen to his feet, pacing the room, as a crass-girlie road movie played on. A crucial point reached, to be interrupted by the commercials and Manfredi grabbed his jacket, and was on his way out.

'Okay, okay,' my voice sounding shrill and needy.

'Seriously Murrey I can't take much more of this,' and he said it like he meant it, like he was about to give up on me.

My inarticulated reasons drove him to exasperation, stopping short at the end of my tongue. I had to do something, so I took a deep breath and offered him some rationale, a few homemade truths.

See it really does not do to go rummaging in someone else's past and definitely not someone you have fallen in love with. For it is easy then to find sullied traces of what went before, unearthing points of jealousy or insecurity. Far better not to delve, not too deep, there's no point in giving each other ammunition. Past suitors are always reprehensible, knowing well my own array of pauses on the line to finding my Man. And I'd try not to be possessive. To love possess then lose out, as entwined we source our origins, nothing comes from nothing.

SHE'D open momentarily to close up all the tighter. No questions asked and another month would slip by. Free-falling to have landed with a bump and it had come as a shock. It didn't make sense to Manfredi, not considering how good things had been between them. A period when his mood had infected all facets of his life. He

177

would hum on his way to the studio, the early spring beams of sunshine soothing and he glided smoothly forward in a current of contentment. Had Manfredi been oblivious to her sensibilities, perhaps he would have understood but everything he had done, he had done with her in mind.

Concentrating in a desperate bid to discover a moment that would enlighten and lead him to some sort of lucid reasoning, Manfredi suspected the letters had something to do with it. Letters from her mother which seemed to jump Murrey into an unknown space.

She left him.

He kept repeating it over and over. She left him nothing but a lingering scent and an unanswered why?

WHY?

The truth was, I hadn't felt so happy in a long time, stamping on every crack in the pavement, running foolhardy under any ladder.

Working in Al's turned out to be fun and relieved Debra and I clicked, my presence failed to threaten her, the way so many best friends can react towards the newcomer.

Straight off I told her I'd been jealous of her that night at Manzoni's.

She said it was unusual. All the years she'd known Manfredi, he'd never lived with anyone. Sure, he'd had affairs, minor skirmishes of the heart but nothing to her knowledge terribly serious.

'Believe me Murrey you're the best thing to have happened to him in a long while. All the years I've known him, I ain't seen the guy so happy.'

Debra was going through a rough period, brave-facing it having been dumped by Tomas. She'd discovered he'd finally left his wife and kids for Dot. Smitten by her unctuous tones, he had asked Dot to front his band, tempting her with notions of fame and glory. I couldn't believe Dot could be so easily taken in.

I did my best to console Debra and offered her a sympathetic ear.

Debra reckoned men were good for one thing and sometimes not even that.

'Give them an inch and they'll claim it's nine.'

To ward off encroaching bitterness, I urged her not to despair and gave her the book I'd thieved, to lift her spirits and bring good luck. Well it had worked for me.

'Love is just round the corner,' I cheered, attempting to humour her.

She dagger-eyed me.

'Ain't no corner, it's a block and one I've been round once too often.'

'Fuck the geometrics at least you've been round it.'

Sure look at me and I ran to the Ladies to mirror face and reflect a moment on past occurrences, corners reached, to then ricochet wildly in haphazard directions, find myself in a new town, with a new man and another letter in the mailbox.

Dearest Murrey,

Thank you so much for the photo of yourself and Manfredi up at the lake. I received it and have sat entranced for hours on end. How beautiful you are and how handsome he is. You make a wonderful couple and I have to admit to a few trickling tears. Perhaps that's me being silly but it's true nonetheless. There you are looking so well and so grown up.

179

I had forgotten you are a young woman now. Stupid really, I expected to see my little girl but there in the envelope was proof, not only of your obvious happiness but also of the time spent apart. It really is a terribly long while since we were together and I feel I have missed out on so much of your life.

Well enough of that, things are fine with myself. Margaret and I are still dancing and we've entered a type of oldie dance league. We are through to the semi-final and enclosed is a photo taken at the last session. By the way Mrs Bunyon passed on last week, I'm sure you'll remember her, you used to hate the way she molly-coddled you!

Lots of love

Mum

My gaze transfixed upon the photo, an instant Polaroid, my mother stood in the centre of some sterile hall, stout. She looked the way women of a certain age get, older, with her waist disappearing in a blue sedate navy dress, a sash draped across her chest and hair drawn back tight in a bun. I showed the photo to Manfredi and he remarked that at last he knew where I got my looks from.

Christ, how I wanted to see her, earn her forgiveness for all the troubles I'd heaped on her. I had dumped every fear, insecurity, failure, doubt, resentment upon her. My poor mama and I thought maybe I'd send a good luck card, for the semis of the dance competition.

It was late in the afternoon, the midday rush over, my shift nearly at an end. A dribbling of customers dawdled, unable to make decisions, constantly changing their minds. My gaze travelled outside, to where a guy was locking his bike to a street pole. He was wearing bicycle clips. A prompter for my thoughts, pulling me from the 'salami, gherkins, onion, no pastrami, gherkins, no smoked turkey, oh heck, why don't I have a little bit of each' sandwich I was making for an obese lady in the corner.

'Hey, is there anybody home?'

Debra dimwits me.

'Sorry, I was just thinking back to when I was a kid.' I slammed a rye cover on top and sprinkled a handful of crisps round the edges of the plate. I could see the woman looking anxiously for me.

'Is anybody homeeeee?' wandering from one room to the next.

It was late in the afternoon. There was no one at home which was puzzling. I yelled in vain, my voice sounding thin in the empty space. I'd just got back from school, home-time, school tie loosened and socks fallen round my ankles, to find the house deserted. No one around, not a soul and disconcerted, I was about to burst out crying, when Bunion's foot appeared mysteriously round the side of the door. She said I was to have tea at hers, cause my mother had gone out with my father.

Bunion lived three doors down and her house smelt like her feet and her husband of beer and she cut some soda bread and slices of ham and cheese and she said she'd treat me and opened a tin of pineapple rings.

Her husband came home, disappointed to find me there and asked what I was doing. Taking a plate of lamb chops from the oven, Bunion replied there's trouble up at the Pogues.

'What do you mean trouble?'

And she was throwing glares toward me, saying she'd tell him everything later and to eat up while his meal was still warm.

'Friggin' headcase if you ask me,' declared Ron Bunion, chewing on the bones and crunched them between his teeth. I asked Bunion if I could go home but she said I'd have to wait till my mother got back.

They sat watching the telly, *The Black and White Minstrel Show*. I wasn't interested, stood by the window, waiting to see if I could catch sight of either of my parents. It was late and I must have fallen asleep on the couch cause my mother was shaking me by my shoulder, telling me to get up.

'Thanks Mrs B, you're very good.'

'What did the doctors say?'

'They're not sure.'

I was drowsy, sleep stuck to my lids, dampening my finger to ease it off.

We walked back down the road silently.

I asked her where Dad had gone.

'Your dad isn't well,' she answered. I asked again and she said she was tired and not be at her all the time.

'Come on,' she said, pulling at my arm, 'I'm famished,' and dragged me home.

Moving forward between the café tables, with a huge sandwich balanced on a tray, I could see the fat lady was fading away. The bicycle remained locked to the pole outside, where a dog cocked his leg in salutation.

'Girl what took you so long?' the cow demanded.

I apologized, stating Al's policy was to serve only products of the highest quality.

She told me I'd blown my tip, I stretched my lips to

extremity, baring my pearly whites and bid her a healthy dose of indigestion.

'Excuse me, miss?'

Pivoting round, I came face to face with Kelly Richards. She was everything I wasn't and she was back.

Kelly beamed down at me with a friendly enquiry. Informed me she was a friend of one the regulars, a guy called Manfredi.

'Manfredi, where'd he get a name like that?' I turned the name over on my tongue. 'Oh yeah, I remember him vaguely.'

Okay it was childish of me to then announce he'd been killed in a freak lightening accident but straight after I did admit it was a joke.

'Just joking Kelly,' and I told her I hadn't seen him in a while.

My delusions brought a frown to her all-American sunshine face and it suited her. I slapped her back as any buddy would. The shock swept across her and I had to sit her down, fan napkins in her face. 'He's fine,' I said. 'Comes in now and again. You want to order something?'

'No . . . no thanks,' she stammered, looking at me like I had two heads. 'Have we met before?' as she stared at me.

'Doubtful,' I replied.

'How d'you know my name?'

She had me perplexed, had I really called her Kelly?

I laid her mind to rest. 'Yeah Manfredi's mentioned you to me.' Cursing myself for having made such a mess and later that evening she called the apartment, to tell tale tattle. There I was sitting across from

Manfredi, my cheeks a resplendent rouge. Caught red-handed.

MANFREDI caught her out and he guessed he should have taken it as one of her warped compliments but instead he blew up.

'I can't believe you'd do that. It's so fucking pathetic.'

Murrey didn't answer, she didn't say anything just sat silently like a scolded child.

'YOU'RE so fucking pathetic,' that's exactly what he said and for the first time ever I'd nothing to say.

This time I couldn't blame my mother, shamed by my own shortcomings, I looked to Kelly.

Now, I don't wish to labour the point but remember, I know a thing or two about kisses. As much passion can be contained in the meekest of lip-brushes as in an open-mouthed deluge. Kelly had returned and in advance, I knew what was coming.

She would look for him, it was obvious, she wanted him. I knew the type of woman she was.

The temperature had risen, boiling point about to be reached and Debra had sent me off to get some ice. We'd run out of cubes in Al's, so I hopped over to the café across the street to ask if I could borrow a bag of theirs. It was an emergency, our cooler on the blink and everyone was getting hot about the collar.

Into the cool café I ventured, with its air-conditioning plus moisturizer and the manageress didn't recognize me. Funny that. She asked if I liked working in Al's and how much I was paid cause she had some vacancies to fill.

'Al's is just an interim thing for me,' I answered, telling her I'd got a huge part in *ER*.

She was flabbergasted, wanted to touch my arm, demanded an autograph.

'Really?' she gasped.

'Yeah,' I announced, 'Sure by the next series my face will be plastered all over the city, on every magazine, paper, subway, bus shelter, you name it.'

Stupefied she was all a fluster, 'Wow, boy-oh-boy, impressive, you know I was once an audience member on *The Jerry Springer Show* and I thought that was cool.'

'No, that's sad,' I informed her.

Humbled, she offered me a large coffee with all the toppings for free and as much ice as I wanted. 'I'll drop the ice bags down to Al's myself. Wait there,' she said and disappeared into the kitchen to get some.

Leant against the dark glass, reflecting outward, my heart on red alert leapt to recognize my man, sauntering down the sidewalk. Manfredi in toeless sandals and shorts, his shirt open, humming. I guessed he was on his way to Al's and hoped he was thinking about me when at that precise moment, he stopped, right outside the café and I inside, hidden behind the dark reflective glass, like some customs official. The expression on his face broadened as she swooped down into view, tall and blonde, so pretty and perfect, like everything was under control, her clothes all matching, her hair thrown back off her face and she hugged him close.

From where I was standing Kelly was back in the picture. I could not hear what they were saying but lip read and I am one-hundred-per-cent certain of the fact that hers brushed upon his.

She pointed to the café, to the glass which I was standing behind and he shook his head, like I never existed. Of course that's how I saw it, how it felt. His face alight, looking at his watch, making a future date and waved her off. I froze, a nauseous feeling swept through me, clogging up my insides and shaking I crossed back over the street to Al's.

Manfredi was there waiting to be served, waved me over, to kiss me, asking if I'd been slacking. Me?

'You're cold.'

I thought I'd mention the fact that I'd seen them, you know get it out in the open. There's no point letting things build up inside.

I said, 'You look happy,' and he told me he'd just run into a friend. A collision of feelings, leading to a combustion and freeze frame, cause I knew I'd have to move on.

We'd reached a pinnacle. There was no other way forward, than the downward descent.

Manfredi turned to me, 'Murrey, you look like you've seen a ghost.'

Spirits abound in the old country, swarming within homes, reeking under the weight of their own personal histories. In the arms of my father by the bedroom window of an evening. I, warm beneath him, my father's gaze, skyward directed, dreaming on stars. He held me tightly to him, the pair of us hoping to spot a shooting one. He described to me the death of a star and how it creates a hole in time and space. A perfectly captured moment of infinity. Doing my best to comprehend and keep my eyes open, but the lids did droop and I would rub them, so that they would open again. I fell asleep in the comfort of his arms, his steady breathing lulling me to dream and when I woke he had gone and I found myself alone in the darkness of the room, tucked beneath Snow White, Disney sheets. He had drawn over the curtains.

Manfredi rose from his bed and drew back the curtains, to view rain clouds passing, checking the time on his radio alarm. Exactly twenty-four hours since the morning before when he had surprised Murrey with a breakfast tray in hand and she, curled up in bed, tried to hide from her daily routine of taking orders. The smell of warm croissants and milky coffee gently woke her.

He had hoped to please her, reassure her, instead she asked if he was suffering from a guilty conscience.

'Can't I just do something nice?'

'What, for the sake of it?'

'Yep,' he said, 'Just for the heck of it.'

Planting the tray on the bed, pissed at her reaction.

'By the way,' he said, 'You got another letter from your mother,' then went to shower.

She stepped in as he stepped out again, passing the bar of soap from his hand to hers. Manfredi quickly dressed, returning to say goodbye as Murrey rinsed soapsuds from out of her hair.

She'd flicked water at him, threatening him with the shower nozzle.

'Will I see you later?' he asked.

'Not sure what I'm doing,' she answered.

Since he'd bumped into Kelly, he had sensed Murrey retreating, clamming up as if scared of something. He didn't get it, everything he did backfired.

He left the apartment, feeling heavy within, as if

knowing something was going to give. The day already hot and humid, a storm threatening the skies. He dragged himself to the studio. Sol was there in a state of anguish.

He'd been caught at a lap-dancing club by his youngest sister, wrapped around a pole. She claimed to be there as part of her therapy treatment.

'She was wearing a wig. I swear Manfredi, I didn't know it was her when I called her over.' Sol shuddered, 'Sick or what?'

'So what did you do?'

'Ach I gave her twenty bucks and left.'

The thought of listening to Sol kvetch on pushed Manfredi back up on his feet and he left the studio and headed over to Lake View, to window shop and clear his head.

Visually arrested outside a secondhand clothes store, Manfredi stalled.

Vagabond Daze and his neck rotated slowly, to be drawn toward a vintage dress, hanging as the centre-piece in the window and immediately Manfredi imagined it on Murrey.

Impulsively he pushed open the door of the shop. The interior empty save for himself and the owner, an elderly man with too few strands of hair, neatly placed over the dome of his liver-spotted head. He sat behind his glass counter, playing on a Gameboy. The old man acknowledged Manfredi with a welcoming nod and croaky invite to feel free to browse.

Removing his glasses, Manfredi's eyes adjusted to the interior. A haze of sunlight heavy with dust, as if suspended in motion, the shop bursting with curios, rails of clothes, small pieces of furniture, a counter of paste jewellery, hat boxes piled high, one upon another, in tiers of diminishing size, like a wedding cake. Lace umbrellas, chests replete with old linen, crochet gloves, empty painted tins, vintage remnants of past decades displayed in splendid chaos.

Manfredi glanced over a rail of similar dresses but the one in the window held his attention.

The dress draped on a tailor's dummy, in what he perceived as mint condition, was light pinkish rose in colour with a delicate floral pattern, tiny ivory buttons down the front. He thought it perfect, it would suit Murrey perfectly.

'Tchuh, stupid machine,' the old man grumbled, shuffling to his feet and inching his way around the counter with the aid of a walking stick. 'You like the dress?'

'I was thinking of buying it for my girlfriend.'

'Nice dress,' chortled the old man, 'Boy is there a story to that dress.'

'That so?'

'Belonged to my wife. God rest her soul. She wore it the day I asked her to marry me, the day of our engagement.'

'Really?'

'Yep. She wore it only the once, called it her lucky dress.'

The old man drew in a large breath, nodding his head, as each nod rewound a year back to the recalled time.

'It was 1945, end of the war and I was feeling lucky. We were on our way home.' He spoke slowly, his voice crackling like an old phonograph recording, 'The ship came into dock, it's name . . . ah I can't remember. It'll come to me, it always comes back eventually, the ship, slow sailing up the Hudson Bay. The docks teeming with people, crowds ecstatic. Families gathered to greet their sons. I was an orphan, expecting no one and Tillie . . . Well Tillie was waiting for a soldier she knew was lost for good. You ever see those news Pathé films kid?'

'Sure.'

'The crowds, the jubilation. Well Tillie stood on the pierside waving a handkerchief, wearing that very dress. I spotted her from the deck and waved back. Don't know why I presumed she could distinguish me, amongst a sea of khaki but she seemed to be waving right at me. Then the gangplanks lowered and a group of us men set off in search of waiting sweethearts or any broad for that matter and what do you know but we ran straight into each other. Tillie and I, bang straight into each other and I held on to that beautiful woman and I knew then and there, this was the woman for me. Madness, it would be like picking up some strange broad and within a couple of days proposing . . . but it worked for us.' The old man smacked his lips together, rubbed his hands in a back-to-business mode. 'Enough with the stories, so you want the dress? Tell you what, I'll let you have ten-per-cent discount, you look like a romantic yourself.'

Manfredi had bought it, the old man wrapping it up carefully in purple tissue paper and gold ribbons and wished Manfredi all the luck in the world. The shop once more empty, the old man hobbled back to one of the chests, raised the lid, took out an identical dress then rehung it on the dummy in the window.

'Schmuck,' sighed the owner, pressing the pause button on his Gameboy.

Manfredi made straight for Al's to catch Murrey

before the afternoon shift. The diner was bustling with the lunchtime trade. Debra flew past him, four plates balanced in her two hands, shooting him a look of disdain.

'Where's Murrey?' he asked.

Debra looked stressed.

'You tell me Manfredi. She was meant to be here over two hours ago. She hasn't shown.'

'What?'

'Your girlfriend has fucked up big time.' She snarled as if Manfredi were to blame. 'I expect at least a courtesy phone call.'

'She said she was working today.'

'Yeah, well, she never showed, I rang twice, got the answer message both times.'

To double bow my running shoes that snugly fit my one-track mind and leave. It was merely a matter of time, the unexpected hit and blew me sideways as a punch. There I'd been, letting down my guard and feeling free in my vulnerability.

This feeling distinct, familiar and my neck tensed up, as if someone was pulling my hair from behind.

And it puzzles me, each and every time, how wrong one can be. It inches inside my stomach, the food of love and I want to retch out this lining, turn over the sheets cause they are so goddamn stained.

It was inevitable, history has a sense of continuation about it, there's no getting away from it.

First sign of trouble and I'm out of there. I call it my 'jerk reaction'. It's always the same, you meet someone new, violin strings trill, till they snap and then the smell of disappointment pervades. It winds its way up my nostrils, to coincide with the realization that it's not just the pair of you, there's a host of shadows lurking.

It was beginning to make sense, or if I thought about it in such terms, it would. I required a justification and found one in Kelly.

Her arrival had the potential to force an ending, with her saccharine intentions, like butter wouldn't melt in her mouth. Kelly and he'd told me she wasn't his girlfriend.

Lie. I'd asked him that time outside the bookstore.

Liar.

Looking for an escape clause, I was twiddling the letter from my mother in my hands, when I heard a familiar tapping sound coming from the bedroom. I stopped to listen. The repetitive rapping insistent and even before I had time to draw up the wood slat blinds, I could see those distinctive bands of colour. My life in black and white. Its dark magpie beak pressed up against the window, my fist raised at the bugger, wanted to punch through the glass, grab that tail-end feather, pluck out its beady eyes, leaving it directionless.

Dressed for work, an ominous feeling rising in my throat. The phone rang, automatically I went to answer it.

'Hello?' I hoped it was Manfredi and I'd warn him of the danger of falling for someone. Especially someone like me. I'd tell him he was right, what he'd said about me, being pathetic and . . .

'Hey, Murrey,' it's been ages,' her slur instantly recognizable, unmistakably Dora.

'Doesn't seem so long,' I replied.

'Whatever . . . anyhow thought I'd let you know I was

back, Zebedi's coming next week. He wants to see you.'

'You told him where I was?'

'Not exactly but . . .'

'Great Dora, I thought we were friends?'

'Hmm, listen, Murrey I need some money . . .'

Call me a bitch, but I slammed down the phone. There was no way I was going to get embroiled in that shit again. The fact she knew where I was intimidated me, though I was pretty certain the Zebedi ploy was a trick. She had used it on me once before, though I didn't doubt she could make things difficult for me. Everything was getting messy. I wanted a way out.

I tore open the letter from my mother and began to read:

Dear Murrey,

I received your card the day of the dance competition, you must have packed it with good luck cause didn't Margaret and myself only step one-two away with the trophy. I'm pleased as punch and only wish you could have been there to witness it. Tom was surely looking down on us that night. I have the trophy resting on the mantelpiece, all shiny and bronzed, it's a sight to behold. There'll be no stopping me now, who knows where it may lead. Rumour has it there is a similar league in the States so you never know, I may be coming over your way!!

I hope you don't mind but I wanted to celebrate and I'm sending you a little something so you can treat yourself. Think of it as an accumulation of all those birthday presents I never got you. So there you are Murrey, take care of yourself.

Big kiss

Mum

Mind? She'd sent me three hundred dollars; so much for the soothsayer magpie. Oh slick-feathered trickster, my guardian angel and I knew the time had come.

Packing my large grey suitcase, listening to Debra on the answerphone asking where I was. I called the ticket-line. Hauled my belongings down the stairs, cursing each step, to hail a cab at the corner of the street.

'Where to lady?'

Then I saw him, Manfredi running with a frown on his face. His lips pressed together, disappearing, one on top of the other, to a mean line and my eyes clouded over.

When my father returned from hospital, he stopped talking. Or he didn't talk to me and mum. I'd been sitting on the step outside the door, waiting for them. There was a small gravel pathway leading to the house, it was not the right surface for hop-scotch, so I sat playing with a colouring book. Not the colour-by-number type, nor the joining-the-dots one. It was a special type Bunion the Onion had bought for me. She'd been up at the house helping out; my mother had got a job in a hotel in the city centre, so Bunion would drop in, or I'd have to go round to hers after school. I'd sort of gotten used to her smell and often she'd buy stuff for me, probably cause she had no kids of her own. There was a small red plastic paintbrush Sello-taped to the front cover and all you had to do was get a glass of water, dip the brush in and paint on to one of the blank pages, then colours would appear, and a picture form, just like that. A magic painting book, but if you weren't careful with the water, if you wet the brush too much, the colours would run, one into the

194

other. So I sat with the red plastic, black thistle brush, making the invisible visible. I wore my best dress. Mum had warned me, I was going to have to be on my best behaviour and I wasn't to get excited she said I had to do everything very slowly when I was around Dad and not to expect too much.

On the step expecting them.

The bus stopped at the end of the street, so whenever I heard the rumble trundle of the No. 16, I'd run to the gate to see if they were getting off. Six buses passed, during which time Bunion had brought me up an egg sandwich and a glass of Lucozade and the colour book was complete and, bored, I had spilt the murky water on to the pages, purposely to mix the colours, as the pictures weren't that interesting and when I heard the seventh bus, off I ran towards the gate, they had to be coming this time.

On my own, I was never allowed to go further than the gate. I understood this but when I saw them, when I saw my dad stepping down off the bus, I didn't care a jot and ran straight out on to the pathway, waving and hollering at the top of my voice.

I was so happy to see him, clasped my arms round his legs, wanting to be lifted up and kissed.

My father . . .

And I have so few memories of him. I can remember his bicycle, his big black bicycle and he'd prop me on the seat and wheel me up and down the pathway on it. It was a Triumph Flyer, I can recall its shape, colour and the bell. It had a bell on it. He wore clips over his trousers and a cap. He would have been about my age, twenty-four.

He used to cycle everywhere.

There is a picture of him with his hair slicked back. Kiss curled at the front. It was taken at some dance or other. He is standing beside my mother, one hand wrapped around her waist, with a cigarette in his other. He looks like a movie star but I guess every daughter thinks that of her father. I found the picture under a loose pile of photos, half hidden in an old biscuit tin, a split-second take on him. This image, it doesn't marry with my own visual memory. It was taken before I knew him. My mother looks anxious, both her hands resting on her belly. See there I was, my little presence already a worry. And he had such beautiful lips and his eyes sparkled. Even in that black and white imagery, there seemed to be so much life inside of him.

He would bring me to the park on the weekends, hold me by my arms and swing me round and round so I'd be sick dizzy and world swirling and sometimes he'd chase me, to scoop me up and kiss me or I'd run up to him like a rock-and-roller dancer and jump up into him.

My mother pulled me away.

To fall in step at her side.

He didn't say anything.

We walked back to the house, he didn't raise his eyes from off the pavement.

He didn't say a thing.

Not even a word.

MANFREDI ran back to his block, his step hastening in pace, meeting the ground to rise up quickly again, the bag at his side, pendulating in rhythm. He arrived panting, a sense of urgency growing within. Pushing the key in the lock, he shoved open the door, calling out her name as he rushed inside, ran from room to room, drawers, cupboards opened and all emptied, devoid of any sense of her. Searched for a note or a clue but she had taken as much of her self as she could, leaving him with nothing more than the photo montage stuck to the wall and her scent. Her smell, it hung in the air, he'd probably just missed her. Desperately he tried to think of places she may have gone and, about to call Debra to ask if she had any bright ideas, he stopped and hit the last number redial.

The last number called, the tone ringing, number ten in the queue, then four, then two.

'Good afternoon United Airlines can I be of service?'

Worth a try and Manfredi hauled himself back down the fourteen flights, out on to the sidewalk, to jump into the first cab he managed to flag down. Leant forward on the edge of his seat and breathless,

'O'Hare, it's an emergency.'

'You got it.' The cabby's obliging foot slammed down on the accelerator, forcing Manfredi to rock back.

The driver glanced at him through the rear-view mirror.

'You okay mister?'

'Sure.'

'Well you look kinda strange to me.'

The last thing Manfredi needed was some rear-seat, taxi confessional.

'Know what mister, you look kinda familiar.'

Manfredi lost in his own thoughts, failed to register a response.

The driver raised her voice,

'Hey mister do I know you? I mean you look kinda familiar?'

'What?'

She caught his attention and he looked toward the mirror to face her. She could only have been about nineteen or twenty, dressed all in yellow, a yellow cap on her head, beneath which straggling straw-blonde hair escaped.

'Yeah, you look a lot like an old boyfriend of mine.'

'Pardon?'

'Yeah, a good few years older than me, he'd carrot hair like you. Hey do I look familiar to you?' She swung round in her seat to face him.

'Never seen you before. Sorry.'

'You remember a night behind the Kmart store, making out on top of rotting vegetables?'

Manfredi couldn't believe it, wished he'd taken the El. Next she'd be accusing him of fathering a child, or passing on some deadly disease.

'See, I remember, cos it was my first time and the guy you resemble, well he weren't no gent.'

Manfredi offered sympathetic glances,

'I was young, we all make mistakes. I thought I understood him. You know this need to continually prove himself.'

'How's that?'

'The guy only had one ball. You have one or two balls?' She was chewing green gum, pulling it out from her mouth.

Manfredi raised two fingers.

'You have a girlfriend?'

He nodded.

'Why you looking so glum.'

'It's complicated.'

'Listen you not happy with her, I'll give you a chance.'

She drove like a maniac, one hand on the wheel, pre-empting lights as if she was racing the clock, till finally swerving over to the kerb and half on it, half off, the dollar lights flashing.

'That'll be forty bucks mister.'

Manfredi reached into his pocket and drew out fifty dollars. She took the notes, went to rummage around in her change bag, then heard him mutter, 'Keep it.'

'Hey and I'm serious if you ever feel like a ride you know who to hail.' She winked at him but already Manfredi was racing toward the entrance of the terminal. Blindly looking in every direction and trying to introduce some logic to his search, airport, destination, ticket, he made straight for the ticket sales. A small row of travellers stood tensely edging forward. Scanning the line and his gaze panned over her before double-taking back. Tapping her feet impatiently, her large cumbersome bag by her side.

He lost all impetus to move, stuck to the spot as a surge of anger ran through him, watched her shuffle forward, in order to leave him the quicker. Steadying himself, Manfredi's shoulders tensed, to breathe in deeply, unsure of what he would say and walked towards her.

Aside her, waiting for an acknowledgement. She jostled him, thought he was trying to queue barge.

'Hey, that was my place.'

'Murrey.' Her eyes wide and blinking at him.

'Murrey,' his voice slightly strained. 'Aren't you going to say anything?'

'Look Manfredi I'm a free spirit I'll wander where I will.'

'Christ, that sounds like a line out of a crappy novel.'

'Yeah, well, maybe it is.'

'So are you going to tell me why you're running away?'

'Actually it wasn't such a crap novel.'

'For chrissakes this is serious.'

His impulse to slap her hard, shake some sense out of her. 'I don't understand what's happened.'

'Why does there always have to be a reason? Look nothing lasts forever, believe me I'm doing you a favour.'

'You're talking bullshit!'

'Yea that's what I do, have you never noticed?'

'Jesus Murrey!'

'Did I never tell you about the time on the Greyhound bus, I was travelling between . . .'

'I don't want to know.'

'See I sat beside this guy . . .'

'Why?'

'This story is kinda sad, he was one of those bums . . .'

'Why?'

'Bill, his name was Bill . . .'

'Murrey what the fuck are you doing?'

'Wanna know the first thing that struck me when I came to the States? How come everyone was looking for a guy called John? The John, get it? It's a bad joke.'

'Answer me.' He grabbed her by the shoulders. His rage mounting, stirring interest from queue members, eager to catch what was happening.

'Stop shouting at me,' she muttered, head hung under the spotlight of attention.

'Answer me.'

'I don't know.'

'That's not good enough.'

She started crying, plump tears rolling down her cheeks.

'Are they the real thing?'

'Fuck you Manfredi.'

'Why? That's all I want to know.'

'He botherin' you darlin'?' A do-gooder teetered on the edge of interrupting. Murrey shook her head, her lips pursed.

He was waiting for an answer, an explanation, a response. Her hands shook so, she plunged them into her coat pocket.

'I . . . I . . .'

'Tell me why?' his voice echoing loudly, unafraid to make a commotion.

'So you and Kelly can pick up from where you left off.'

'Kelly? What has she got to do with anything?'

'Yeah, like there was nothing between you two, like how come she's expecting to walk back into your life?'

'That's all in your fucked-up mind and you know it.'

She didn't reply, he didn't want her to stop talking, to ignore him.

'I don't get it. I love you. Murrey. Say something. Please.'

The do-gooder muttered renewed support for Murrey, 'They're all the same Sweetie.'

Manfredi turned on the lady's neighbourliness, 'Just butt out.'

He couldn't fathom what was happening.

'What are you playing at?'

She stopped sniffling and quietly she said,

201

'Always asking questions, wanting to know everything. Okay you wanna know the truth?' She paused, her eyes darting from the ceiling to the floor unable to meet his. '. . . I used to work in the Weiner Circle selling roses to romantic couples. Sold you and Kelly one. And . . . and though I'm good at bullshitting, my real talent is theft. You know watches, wallets, Psions . . . information is real valuable these days. I was staying with a crackhead, fuck-up. We used to hang together . . . work together, Manfredi . . .'

'You expect me to believe this?'

Again with her stories.

'Why are you doing this?'

Murrey had reached the top of the queue, Manfredi stood staring at her, wondering if he was missing the point.

'Are you trying to tell me you don't love me?'

She didn't reply, he repeated the question, daring her.

'Answer me.'

Sighing loudly, she turned to face him.

'Okay I don't love you.'

'Bullshit.'

Her eyes met his,

'No, really Manfredi, I don't love you.'

'Excuse me ma'am, are you here to collect a ticket?' enquired the ticket operator, her tone over-polite. Murrey spun round and when she turned back Manfredi had gone.

If Manfredi had done something wrong, if he had made some major error he could have understood. If able, he gladly would have taken the blame, at least then he could comprehend her motives for leaving. For him it would be easier to deal with. He'd turned on his heels to walk away, telling himself it was just another game.

She would follow him out of the airport and somehow end up back at the apartment later. He tried hard to convince himself of the possibility.

To be in love with an impossibility, it didn't bode well, it never had. Manfredi cursed his gullibility, so easily swayed. If he understood anything it was that he had lost her.

He returned from O'Hare only to find a dope-fiend in his apartment going through his drawers. His presence scared her and she'd taken a flick-knife from out of her jacket to feebly threaten him, whilst backing out of the place. He called the cops and by the time she'd made it down the stairs, the elevator being out of order, they were waiting to take her away.

And all through the night her words stormed his mind, going over and over what she had said, what she had meant, trying to figure if any of it really mattered to them. Excuses, excuses, and she told him she no longer loved him. Wrenching herself from a love he had never had cause to doubt.

The following morning, still searching for a reason, wishing he could have woke and found her there beside him. To sniff the pillow where she once lay, yearning to breathe easy again. It was time to get up and face the day. Half-hearted efforts made, limbs half stretched, this wasn't really happening. Sat on the edge of his bed, Manfredi's body slumped over, his back bent and beneath the base he caught a glimpse of pink. A small pink envelope with posies on the edge, old fashioned and torn. He picked it up, turning it over to read a return address.

Itching to have reached this point, to have travelled this dreamland and with my mother's money in my pocket, I had an overbearing sense of purpose.

I had turned my back on Manfredi, my face tensed up, felt so ashamed. I could see his reflection in the glass above.

He looked hurt.

And I thought it only right to tell him, it was only fair he knew, even if it served merely to clarify my own state and I believe the following to be tinged by truth, whatever that may mean.

See all that stuff before, it didn't really happen, well not the way I explained.

Sometimes you've got to tweak the imagination a little, to make things more palatable, so I elaborated, embellished. I wanted to make it interesting, mask myself in some semblance of adventure. Besides these days only the astonishing is believed. The truth lay below in murky waters and those love run-ins, they may have led me astray but in the end I was delivered straight to him, as a wish coming true.

It does happen, a possibility winks across at you, a small burgeoning adventure just waiting to be claimed.

You usually do get what you want.

Manfredi told me he loved me, wrapped me in his arms and drenched me in him. Almost like a first kiss, eager to chase a tongue upon a lip and taste a love of sorts, his sweetness and pungency washing over me.

And I felt zero, as a circle complete.

He had sent me reeling, right back in time, real time, but this wasn't some movie you pay four dollars to waste an afternoon at.

Love?? . . . You cast out wide and then you slowly haul yourself back in, cause the longer you look at him the stranger he becomes.

He told me once I smelt of wild roses. I used to sell them to wandering lovers or the guilty minded.

Recalling that fateful evening, outside the gallery, sneaking a glimpse of him behind the glass and putting it down to another case of wishful thinking, I retreated back into the shadows.

Kept him in mind, till he reappeared before me, catching sight of him, strolling through Lincoln Park with Kelly, on the cusp of an affair. I sidled over, a posie offered in my hand and they responded by taking pity, aided by my picturesque image, shivering in the cold of a late-autumn evening. I was very good at shivering.

'Which do you think it should be Manfredi?' and she pointed to the different clusters of flowers, heaped randomly in my basket.

'Ah but we should leave it to the professional,' he replied, indicating myself and I chose for him, so that he should think of me when looking at her. Kelly, and the pair of them, like they had just walked out of an advertisement. As I pinned the bunch to her coat lapel, my left hand darted into her bag to lift what I could. Quick as you like. He stood to her side, muttering something I failed to overhear.

What the Dickens was going on and for a moment I thought I was done for.

'Oh thank you sir, very kind sir,' doffed my hat and humbly accepted his ten bucks, even though the pin flowers were worth no more than four at a push. Then off I rushed, embarrassed by their obvious contentment.

He said I smelt like wild roses when in truth I smelt of loneliness.

Dora was waiting for me back at the flat. Dora, my one real friend, the sad fact being the pair of us were total losers, the only two negatives not to make a positive.

'What you got?' She needed fixing, she was always in need of a fix.

The deal was I did a bit of business for her each day, so I could stay at her place. She would cream off what she could in the form of cash, cards and trinkets easy to pawn, but most of the stuff went to Dino, to whom she was heavily indebted. Dino ran a racket or two, burglary being one of his more lucrative ventures.

Dora wasn't so pleased with the Psion, 'What the fuck good is that?'

Think Dora, think? It's full of addresses and numbers, information is real valuable these days and she looked at me like I'd lost it, waving the phone directory in my face. Okay, I'd lifted it on purpose. See I knew his name and I wanted his number. It was a fancy on my part and then the next day, under cover of the Theatre Royale, I waited, expectant of his arrival. Sol had been very helpful. It was an old-time movie theatre where they played arty films, the type hardly anyone goes to.

A couple days later in Al's, eye-tag, dilated flirtations,

his eyes large and clearly defined, I could see myself in them. Unfortunately next thing was, I saw Kelly arrive and I left quickly, fearing she'd recognize me, put two and two together.

As for the rest, well it really did happen and I felt like the luckiest person alive. Until the time when everything began to fall in on top of me. My mother's letters, pulling me this way and that, his persistent questions, Kelly's arrival, Dora's call.

Worse still, all of them excuses.

Worst of all, the love I felt for him.

It was like I had stepped into a whirl of distorted sceptres and was vacillating on the brink of submergence. I reverted to type and did what I always do.

To pre-empt and bail out alive, as a form of self-preservation.

See, from every chance of love, I fled.

It's not a constant thing, this love malarkey.

My comforter forsaken and left fishlike on an empty, low-tide shoreline, spasms of life decline. I only ached for a kiss everlasting and clouded sky racing, retracing every back alley ventured down, I . . . him more than ever.

HER mother, no different from any other, had grappled with such familiar fears; that her daughter would grow up to be a replica of herself or worse, the child would grow up to be someone else.

Mrs Pogue woke early, a fragment image in her mind of a picture on a sideboard, a child on skates with her dad. Strange how time catches up on you. She took her large mare-like hands and ran them through grey faded hair, to rub her eyes and glance towards the curtained windows, to where a glint of morning light eased its way over the patterned carpet. She pulled her dressing-gown tight about her, beneath, a crumpled nightdress of cotton white, to greet the day in a long-held routine; to wash, dress, to Morning Ireland on the radio, the kettle on the boil. Two slices of brown cut, ready to be popped in the toaster, honey on the table, to smear some early sweetness. Then out into the hall, to check the post and collect the milk from off the doorstep. She stopped by the hall mirror, licked the top of her index finger and ran it over her eyes, waiting for the familiar sound of the black, iron gate to creak open. The door unlocked, its chain pulled back, home sweet home, foot-wipe mat, and greet the milkman on his rounds.

'Good morning Mrs Pogue,' he calls out to her, 'And isn't it a fabulous morning.'

Indeed for the summer approaching and the sky blue smelt fresh and full of promise.

To chat idly for five minutes, allowing for the extra paid for home deliveries and he whispers, con-spiratorially, about No. 17's haemorrhoids and the effect they are having.

A pint of milk in hand and the creak of the black gate, the black gate creaking and out of the morning blue, to rub her eyes in disbelief and recognize her daughter coming up the pathway and the bottle falls, to smash on the gravel, her eyes flooding as the postman dithers, making glib comments about spilt milk.

$$\pi r^2$$

'What time does your flight leave?'.

'5.40 p.m.,' murmured Manfredi, exact in his reply. He'd already told Debra three times.

He was tense, wishing once more he'd taken the El direct to the airport. They were running half an hour late, speeding down the Kennedy Expressway in Debra's clunked-out Chevrolet. She was concentrating on the road, the driver behind, attempting to overtake, was hooting for Debra to switch lanes.

'I bought you these for the flight.' Debra reached into the pocket of her jeans and threw over a packet of sleeping pills.

'You needn't have.'

' In case you get seated next to a real creep.'

'For use on them or me?'

'Both.'

The car pulled up right outside the terminal.

'Do you have time for a coffee?'

It had gone four. Manfredi shook his head.

'I'll get a cart,' announced Debra, throwing Manfredi the keys to remove his luggage.

She disappeared for several minutes, arriving back with a trolley and a couple of Starbuck coffees.

'I better move before I get busted.'

Manfredi nodded, he wanted to be on his own now. 'I should go check in.'

Time to say goodbye and Debra threw her arms around him,

'Take care.'

'See ya Deb.'

'Hey before I forget . . .' and reaching her arm through the open window, to the glove compartment, she took out a present.

'It's for the flight. Thought you may enjoy it.'

Manfredi slipped a giftwrapped book into his bag.

'Thanks, thanks a lot Deb.'

'You sure you making the right decision?'

'No,' he replied honestly.

'I'll miss you Manfredi,' she yelled, 'Oh and bon voyage,' flicking her shades down on to her nose and waved him off, watching after him, as he disappeared inside the terminal.

Manfredi made his way to the check-in, slightly anxious in case he had cut it too fine, only to be told there was a delay. No need to have hurried, air traffic controllers were on strike. Apparently a recurring problem and although the air rep was apologetic, she couldn't say how long the delay would be, insisting they were doing their best. Damn and he thought maybe it was a sign. It wasn't meant to be, he wasn't meant to go, quelling his intuition with the fact that she expected him and would be waiting for him. It wasn't as if she'd forced the decision on him, freely he'd made up his own mind, the move would do him good. Initially he was excited by the prospect of starting afresh, in a new place, the two of them together. Yet, as his departure drew nearer, his own uncertainty grew. His reservations mounted and reassuring himself this was natural, he knew if things didn't work out, he could always come back.

Everything seemed to be going wrong. Manfredi went to sit in a bar, passing the spot where he'd last seen Murrey, the year before.

I HAVE returned, to where I started from. The streets of my childhood and it seems I had to go such a distance just to get here. Sitting on the front step of the small red-brick terrace I share with my mother, reflecting on that time. It is a year since I have seen Manfredi.

My mother is inside, probably in the kitchen making drop scones or laying the table, she is keeping busy and twice already has poked her head around the net curtain, to check on me. I wave a good morning to our neighbour Mr Johnson, the mini-cab driver, off on his daily journeys to and from the airport, trafficking people to destinations and he could tell you a thing or two, if you had the time to listen.

'Grand morning it is Murrey.'

We are hoping for a good summer.

He gets in his Ford parked outside our gateway and he does so like to rev his engine, before releasing the clutch and moving off. Anyhow, I have sensed my mother's furtive presence behind me. The vermilion red of her nearly new cardigan flashes as a warning. We picked it up in the church jumble sale last Sunday. It suits her well, matches the colour in her cheeks. She is anxious for me. Mothers are the incarnation of every child's anxiety.

It is overcast, but I hope it will lift and a blue sky beckon. The clouds move steady and my head is full of cirrus thoughts. It's 9.00 a.m. and skyward gazing, I search out flight paths and count every plane that passes. I try to decipher if they are coming or going. The tips of my fingers are tinged green and between them is a flat blade of freshly picked grass. I have creased it down the middle and whistle through it as I sit patiently.

If I turn my neck to the right, I stare a dead end straight in the face. Dublin Corporation have built a low brick wall to divert the mounting flow of traffic. Now kids from the local school hang out in the pedestrian passageway on their breaks, smoking cigarettes and stealing kisses off one another.

They brim over with attitude, inflated by the certainty of youth and sometimes I hear them brazenly banter about how they will right the wrongs of the world, pronouncing thoughts as if they were somehow original.

Facing me is an identical row of houses.

Mrs O'Brien likes to stand out. She has given her front yard over to the theme of a paradise island. Her front door is fuschia coloured, the small enclosure landscaped with palm trees, ferns and an assortment of strong-coloured flowers. Beneath the front room window is a tap, cleverly disguised as a miniature waterfall. It blends well with the pebbledash front which she had to struggle to retain, due to the uproar from the local residents' committee. She turns on the tap in the height of summer and water trickles down into a small goldfish pond. Ingeniously, she has painted a sunset on her blinds, so on a summer evening it creates quite a picture. She claims to have been inspired by a TV programme and her *pièce de résistance* is an Asiatic looking gnome, his hand pointing upward. He calls to me from across the street, 'De plane, de plane. Eeet's coming.'

To my left is the open road, it cuts across perpendicular, ready to take me either direction and
behind me is the past.

Slate clean, one should not look to the past. I mean it's
physically understood, your neck can only twist so far.
Yet all of us, we swivel owl-like, catching glimpses of
those milestone memories that zip by. Those most
untrustworthy of recollections, mischievously mercurial, rendering reality a dense mass of half-truths.

See what mattered was that first deceit. It hung heavy
on my eyelids and grew as a skin, protecting me from
ever moving forward, while at the same time becoming
my driving force. A phantom love to which I clung, as
the only real thing in life, skirting over the fact that it
was dead but not yet buried.

We are all of us waiting for something and then, when
it arrives, when we have met with our desire, need,
want, whatever it is we have yearned for, it goes. It
comes and it goes, for that is life. To come, to go, to
change.

If this doesn't make sense it doesn't really matter, in
the greater scheme of things it's barely audible.

Anyhow as my mother always said, it will all come
out in the wash.

Ninety degrees, whiter than white, about as far as
my neck can twist and excuse my frankness but I'm
looking straight at you, ready to come clean.

CUTTING it too fine and she had warned him.

Manfredi rushed through passport control to the

gate, looking upward through the glass ceiling into a falling dusk. He'd always preferred flying at night, thought it afforded a strange sense of security.

His flight was called, his fellow passengers rising out of their seats, gathered together their belongings, to swarm about the gateway. Quickly he grabbed a selection of magazines and candy, before taking up his position at the tail end of the queue. Slow moving and going through the motions as if on automatic pilot he shuffled forward, all the way to row 45.

The passenger in the aisle unbuckled his belt to let Manfredi slip across to the window seat. He had obviously come from a convention, his name-tag still pinned to his suit announcing him as P. Lemass. They exchanged courteous nods of acknowledgement and then the fellow disappeared beneath the issued headphones. There was no hint of any forthcoming conversation and Manfredi assumed the following seven and a half hours were safely his own.

Watching the final passengers embark, Manfredi's heart thumped, last-minute decisions taken. Had he done the right thing, was he doing the right thing and he sank back in his seat, to take a deep breath. He eased off his shoes and wiped his face with the warm white towel the air hostess handed out. The video screen lit up in front, the safety drill enacted, orange jacket beneath his seat, oxygen above, the wheels gathering speed, engines roaring and pressed gently back against his chair, to be suddenly airborne.

Manfredi popped his ears, missing the pilot's exact estimation of height, excited now to be on his way. He'd made it, he wasn't sure he would, dithering in the airport deliberating over his course of action.

*

He had called Kelly from the airport to say he'd be delayed.

'Ughh,' waking her from a deep sleep, 'Who is it?'

'Me.'

'Manfredi what is it? Have you changed your mind?'

'There's a delay.'

She sounded disheartened, shaking herself awake.

'I knew this would happen. I told you, you were cutting it too fine.'

He could hear the frustration rising in her voice.

'I know, I'm sorry.'

'You're always sorry, I mean why bother coming at all?'

Her twin sister was getting married to a Parisian composer and the plan had been for both to attend.

'You'll miss the wedding. You knew how much I wanted you to be here.'

'Look Kelly, I'm sure I'll make it over.'

'You were meant to be here weeks ago. It's one excuse after another with you Manfredi.'

'What?'

'Face it, you haven't let go of her.'

'Not that again.'

'Fuck it, I've had it with you.'

'Kelly, I'll do my best to get there. I promise, even if I have to go via someplace else. I promise . . . I . . .'

'Forget it, forget us. Really I've had enough.'

He heard the receiver clink, she had put down the phone on him.

Kelly was right of course. If he'd really wanted he could have arranged things differently. Kelly had been expecting Manfredi to arrive for the past three weeks. Events conspired, preventing him from making a clean break, ends to be tied and ties to be broken, but at last Manfredi felt he had got on top of everything. He had sworn to her that he would definitely, for sure, be there at the end of the coming week. He'd promised he wouldn't let her down and would make it over in time for the wedding.

Kelly's words rang in his ears, the flight delayed and his gaze had reverted to the monitor above, blinking destinations and he recognized it was an actual possibility. He could try and redeem his ticket, fly in someplace else.

Manfredi and Kelly had got back together almost immediately after Murrey left. He hadn't intended to, it had just happened. He couldn't bear being on his own and it was easy. It was comfortable. Their relationship an ongoing affair, that kept, with very little effort on either side, going on. Then three months back, sitting on the terrace of a late-night bar, sipping martinis, Kelly announced her latest job transfer. This time she was off to Paris, to set up a branch office, her contract lasting a minimum of a year.

'Look you know I'm not into long-distance relationships . . . and I thought . . . You wanna come with?' She awaited his response, expected him to take a while, weigh up the implications but his reply was immediate.

'Yeah.'

'You'll come?'

'Sure.'

'You're sure?'

'Yeah.'

Then and her timing was perfect . . .

*

Midday, at his apartment on the Wednesday just gone and surrounded by boxes, Manfredi had been rummaging through the cupboard beneath the sink. He was waiting for the removal men to arrive, the remains of his belongings stacked, ready to be put in storage. He'd spent the morning sweeping up memories, checking his stuff had been labelled correctly. He hadn't suspected he'd accumulated such an amount of dross, bags of it heaped in the far corner, ready to be chucked or dropped off at the Salvation Army. He'd gone from room to room, looking afresh at the place, the stains of time streaking the walls, realizing he'd actually miss it.

Knelt down by the sink, he pulled out a bag, the name of the shop emblazoned across it, Vagabond Daze. He saw the package, the faded tissue paper and carefully he reached inside and unwrapped it. The dress he'd bought for Murrey. The one she'd never worn. He stood up, the dress unfolding in his hands, when the phone began to ring.

He didn't feel like talking and chose to ignore it, waiting for the answerphone to intercede . . .

'Hello Manfredi . . .'

Her voice sounded hesitant, as if she half suspected he may be there. There was no mistaking it and he turned, neck straining at an angle, to face the empty shelf where the answerphone lay.

The sound of her struck a chord, at an all-familiar pitch. She hoped he was fine, that things were going well for him and that she thought about him a lot, probably too much. She was rambling and said if he was there, he wasn't to pick up, cause then she'd feel like an idiot and maybe he would too. She said she'd changed, but in a good way and how much she'd like to see him. Not that it was possible, or even probable, but she thought she ought to tell him. She said she'd had this dream where she'd been hiding out in a box, when a huge hand had just reached inside, scooped her out, hurling her through the air at such a rate she was almost flying, like horizontal bungi-jumping and cause she was dreaming, she could see herself moving from one shadow state to another, as if caught inside a camera, jumping from frame to frame and then, she had landed. She landed safely, though a little shaken and her knees were scuffed but she was okay.

Beeps signalling the end of the message, interrupted her, finishing the one-sided conversation. He waited to see if she'd call again, she did.

'Hey Man what I really wanted to say was, I've been doing some cranial spring cleaning and there are some things I can't quite chuck without acknowledging, certain things I thought you should know . . .'

THAT time when I met Manfredi, my disintegration had already set in and I rushed at him, bulldozed over him, just hoping to make some sense of it all. A cry was surfacing, an internal tremor as I choked on red meat sobs.

The whole of my insides were rancid with feeling and devastated, I could not function, I had not the strength to continue. Stumbling blindly forward, in ever-decreasing circles. I kept bleeding, spoiling everything in sight. My eyes reddening and the only release I had was the thought of punishment, of him, of how I could punish him.

Because it meant hurting myself. I thought it was a normal requisite of love. He had my heart, the whole of me. I wanted to be on his conscience and make a lasting imprint.

To admit this and it's taken its toll, all I ever had.

I could see no alternative, my legacy in my palm, my neck aching and well practised, I wasn't going to take chances.

For a love mercurial?

A love as constant as the stars, as constant as kisses, but what exactly does that mean?

When I look to the heavens, shots ring out, as stars burn up, as coal to ash, and after all of everything, every feeling, felt, fled, I am still as I was.

I used to believe I was born almost raw, missing several layers of skin. My mother, god bless her, thought things would sort themselves out, but they didn't.

See I wanted to tear a layer of his skin from off of his back, to clothe myself, for the longer I stood, the colder I became. I wanted to get under his skin in my search for home. Ill fitting, for I had changed since that first time, keyholed innocent eyes, when love withered before me.

My father used to take me to the park, to feed the ducks, stale breadcrumbs in a brown paper bag. I'd send him Valentines, stick-people images, something to hang flesh on. My hand held in his and it was warm and his clench not so tight as my mother's was, and we walked at my pace, not as when I was with my mother who rushed so, pushing my feet to trip-trop. He would stand behind the swings and raise the seat in the air, to a great height in my mind, my small legs stretched out, outward, cupped under, backwards, higher, higher, my safety net pushing me out into the world and falling back into his arms. My first bicycle, stabilizers and his hand on my back, furiously peddling, back-peddling, back in time to when he held me on his lap, bouncing me, baby bouncing and then his legs would fall open and I would fall through to be caught and hoisted back up and even I could not keep him.

When Dad came back from hospital, he had changed irrevocably.

My mother had to go out and work again.

Kissing the mayhem, my lips quivering. It was an accident. That's what was said, well we wanted him buried properly, couldn't be leaving him in any old limbo.

My knee grazed, grit-studded, the compulsion to announce the latest wound. Mother was working and Bunion would pop by now and again, to keep an eye on me. I had reached the age of understanding and knew well things had changed but couldn't quite put my finger on it. My father would rest up in the shed, in preference to the sitting room, even when the fire was lit.

Playing in the yard, wearing a secondhand pair of rollerskates Bunion had recently bought for me. She said they'd belonged to one of her nieces, who'd outgrown them and I was delighted, looking down at them like they were glass slippers. Red straps on steel casing and there I was dashing the fifteen foot to the back door of the yard and back again, over uneven paving. So I saw it coming, this slip-up, trip-up, down on my knee, the one I always fell on, to reopen old wounds and instinctively felt like bawling. Red droplets, easing down my calf, aided by my squeezing.

Hopping for real over to the shed and I knew my father was there, from the hammering going on, though I'd been told not to disturb him.

'You mustn't be disturbing your father, in heaven's name leave the man alone, unless it's an emergency.'

This was, to me, an emergency, the need for attention, to pull on the doorknob.

To suddenly stop in his hammering and look at me scared, like I'd done something awful with him half-way up a ladder, hammer in hand, nails in his mouth.

Hook, line and sinker and I caught him out.

'I fell,' I explained.

Him looking down at me.

'My knee, it's bleedin,' I elaborated. 'My knee.'

I pointed to it, but he didn't say a word, his mouth all nailed up.

'Has the cat got your tongue? What?'

Slamming the door with intent, the useful good for nothing and I half skated, half hopped down to Bunion's, who having just been shopping, made me a strong cup of cocoa and offered me a choice of Kimberly, Mickado or Coconut Cream.

Indecisive, I chose one of each.

Biscuit crumbs down my front, Bunion's only a hop and a skip away, cocoa breath, milk-brown moustache lipped.

'I'll be off so Bunion,' says I, with my knee newly plastered, leaving her to skin the potatoes for her husband's dinner, the skates still on my feet and off I went.

My mother had come back from work, her coat hung over the banisters. She was up in her bedroom changing, to slip into the chequered, nylon zip-up overall, ready to make our tea.

221

To go up under her feet, wiping the sides of my mouth, so as not to be letting on I'd been snacking.

'Murrey, go on out to your father, tell him his tea will be ready in a minute.'

And I'm not exaggerating, not by a long yard, the rollerskates abandoned, to tippy-toe over to the shed and take him by surprise.

I was looking through the keyhole.

We used to play peekaboo. He'd cover his face in his hands and then draw his palms apart. Peekaboo and I'd laugh, I was suppressing a giggle even then. I was thinking of bursting in on him and giving him a fright.

His back turned to me, what was he up to?

In the name of God. The workbench all tidy, everything had been put away. Peeking in at him, the ground slipped from beneath his feet.

Was that any way to be acting in front of a child?

I stood in front of the door and could see his legs dangling, twitching. He was a great dancer my father, foot tapping to the music, had his sights set on America.

Craning my neck to see further, outside, peeking in at him swinging, and squinting upward, his plaid jumper, head bent over and the rope around his neck.

Mr Bunion was right, he had a crazy head on him.

Sure what was I to do?

To open the door and pull at him, to come down and not be play-acting, to wrap my arms around his legs and tug hard, to come down and stop this silence right now, the shed door swinging open and my mother in the kitchen, her head stuck out the window and was calling us in for tea.

*

My father told me America was the land of dreams and he never woke up again.

And even I could not keep him, I could not keep him.
   You could have passed me through a mangle and I'd still be moist.

Perhaps my father's dreams dashed on my arrival. Or maybe I had nothing to do with it and sometimes, this, for me, is the hardest. That I wasn't even part of the equation but then you can never really know about these things. My mother bore the brunt. Of course she had harboured visions of grandeur, that one day she would be swept off her feet and carried to a life better than the one lived. She used to call him her dreamer, her useless, good-for-nothing, waster.

PERCHED on the edge of the tatty leather armchair, covered in plastic, ready to be put into storage, Manfredi had listened to Murrey's message recorded, played back, taken aback, his thoughts colliding, past and present, tensed up.
   He pushed his fingers through his hair, lifted himself to full height, a year since he'd heard her voice and then wiped his hands over his face. The dress lay crumpled on his lap, his initial response to chuck it on the charity pile changed and he'd decided to send it to her.
   The removal men were banging at the door, he could hear the loud raucous laugh of the head guy. He let them in, then left them to load up the elevator and went to take a shower. The flow of water soothed him, all the while thinking about her. There had been times

when he thought he had lost her forever, when he never wanted to see her again, loathed her, hated her and wept for her.

Drying himself off, a towel wrapped round his middle, his reflection staring back, a razor in his hand and he shaved slowly.

Expected in Paris at the end of the week, when in the nick of time she had called, touched a raw nerve, sending him this way and that, to splash water on his face and cover a cut with a torn piece of tissue. And again Murrey was right for Kelly did recognize her, from the photo montage which he had kept for a while, when he'd been hopeful of her return.

None of it really mattered. He couldn't believe Murrey thought it would make any difference.

In front of the looking-glass Manfredi wondered if he had changed. His curls now closely cropped, another line or two etched around the edges of his eyes. He dressed quickly, towel dried his hair, then pulled on a pair of charcoal linen trousers and indigo blue shirt, checked his reflection one last time. He looked good, in a relaxed carefree manner which seemed to unconsciously fall together. The removal guys were finishing up, the final load going down in the elevator and Manfredi followed the last of his belongings to ground level.

The morning summer rays shone and standing on the sidewalk he had let them soak into him. Under his skin, as if by osmosis, she had changed him. She had definitely and indelibly marked him, her habits, notions, laughter and godawful singing. In everything a past lingers. We hoard our memories in our daily attire, interweave into everything present: phrases, looks, gestures and all cuckooed away.

He had mailed her the dress then doubled back on himself to drop by on Al's.

Only Al's wasn't Al's anymore.

He spotted Debra inside, overlooking the smooth running of the place, exuding a proprietorial air. She waved through the glass at him and then made her way outside, past a small crowd of people waiting to be seated.

'Hey what d'you think?'

Manfredi had been impressed.

'Debra it's great, better than great . . .'

'Yeah not bad. Hey, tomorrow is the grand opening. You are coming?'

'Sure.'

They'd been open unofficially for the past week.

Manfredi admired the new sign above the door. The old painted sign had been removed and replaced by '*Sol's*' in large-script letters.

'I thought you two were gonna call it "The Last Resort".'

'We decided that would suit a late-night club better.'

Looping Manfredi's arm, she pushed back through the door and led him inside, the bell tingled.

'Couldn't get rid of it. Something old, something new.' Debra explained, hands proudly by her side, surveying the place, as if looking anew through Manfredi's eyes.

Unrecognizable, all wood and brash colours, a bookcase along the back wall, small private booths, high stools and low sofas, armchairs and a piano. More a front room than a diner. Centrepiece was an old ornate cabinet slowly revolving, upon which rested a variety of cheesecakes.

And in an ad-hoc way it did fit together.

'Fredi,' cried Sol, his head popping round the kitchen door; he wiped his hands on a tea towel, then threw it over his right shoulder.

Everything seemed to have happened so quickly. Sol had quit the conference business to become joint proprietor and head chef of what was bound to be an institution.

'Note the quality of the serviettes.' Sol pushed one beneath Manfredi's nose.

'Three-ply and printed. You don't get quality like this in those franchises.' White napkins with '*Sol's*' printed in fine script. 'And the plates, the cups and mugs.'

He was radiant with a proud boyish grin.

'Sit down. You hungry, I hope you're hungry?' and he left Manfredi to go and rustle up something.

Sat with his back to the wall, no mirror to peer into, Manfredi forced his gaze outward, to collide with Debra's raised eyebrows, having been waylaid by a yapping customer within earshot.

'I'm standing behind this guy and he's purchasing like ten bottles of shampoo . . .'

'Oh yeah was there a special offer on?' she asked.

'Dunno but he's counting out this bag of dimes, taking his time what's more. Anyway get this, he doesn't have it in change, like a rational human would put one shampoo to the side, don't you think?'

'Exactly.' Debra feigned interest, with just the right amount of enthusiasm.

'So what do you know, only then, like after counting the dimes for a solid five, the guy took out a hundred-dollar bill.'

'Jesus.'

'Yeah, but the point is, the guy didn't have a hair on his head. Now do you get it?'

'No kidding, a baldie,' and she smirked before quickly availing of a conversational exit clause, 'Did you want your eggs turned sir?'

'Whatever Debra. Excuse my asking, but is Debra your real name?'

She stretched her smile for that extra 15%, told him she'd another customer waiting and would be right back. Flashing a snarl at Manfredi, she leant down to whisper, 'Some things never change.'

She left in the customer's order, then sank down into the seat opposite Manfredi's and lit up a cigarette,

'I half expected you'd stop over.'

'Couldn't hold out till the opening.'

'Everything okay?'

'Yeah, the removal men came by this morning. The place is now deemed officially empty.'

'And Kelly?'

Manfredi paused,

'She called just now.'

'Oh yeah, what she say?' Debra blew out a smoke ring. He didn't have to explain anything.

'Ah, so *she* called.'

'Yeah she just called.'

Debra stubbed out the cigarette.

'What you going to do?'

'The right thing.'

'What's the right thing Manfredi. I mean do you really love Kelly?'

She caught sight of a customer calling her over, 'Better get back to work. We'll talk later.'

She had ruffled her fingers through his hair, before planting a kiss on his forehead, then left, almost colliding with the arrival of a Sol double-deluxe pastrami sandwich.

Cruising at an altitude lost over the Atlantic, it was dark and tuned to the classical station Manfredi's head pressed up against the window, looking out at the night sky. Supper had been served, a small tray of compartmentalized food, piping-hot sustenance and a bottle of twist-cap wine, chewed, digested and swallowed as small thoughts.

Most of the passengers were watching the main movie. Manfredi had seen it before. It always happened on long-haul flights and he'd be stuck with having to watch some third-rate documentary about scuba diving off the coast of the Red Sea or the communication skills of dolphins.

In the hope of killing time Manfredi gulped back the sleeping pills then reached down for his bag and opening it, took out Debra's gift.

Unwrapping it he was surprised to find a well-read book, the spine riddled with creases and he guessed Debra must have started reading it and became engrossed. He turned it over in his hands. The front cover had a coffee stain on it and he bent it back and flicked through the pages. It was then he noticed a small sketch, scrawled on the title page, an imperfect heart with what he assumed were wings, beneath which was written, 'Love is . . .' and following the dots he turned the page over to read, 'the closest I ever came to flying'.

He closed the book abruptly, to look again at the title and kicked himself for not recognizing it straight away, *Anatomy of a Kiss*. Laughing to himself he began to read.

*

Drowsing off he fell into a heavy sleep and woke feeling leaden, having to pull himself back into the present. The plane had landed. His muscles cramped, his neck at an acute angle and he rubbed his eyes to stretch the lids, aching to remain firmly shut and surrender to her pull. She had crept inside his head again and danced behind his lashes, coaxing him on. To have heard nothing from her for a year and it felt like he had merely been wading through the intervening period.

Overcome by the prospect of seeing her, Manfredi's tiredness dissipated and he closed the cover of the book lying open on his lap, not quite finished, but fairly certain of how it would end and he pushed it down into the bottom of his bag, along with all his other stuff, eager now to disembark.

Last Minute Wishful Thinking

I can't help it, but this morning, I woke with a feeling, an image in my head, like one of those trailers for a forthcoming movie, and made room for it to run through my mind.

There's a young woman, not the American dream of the girl next door, but a bit more, I dunno, quirky. Not so clean cut and simplistic. She is wearing a summer floral dress, short sleeves, buttons down the front, her legs bare but lightly tanned, hair loose and falling free about her face. It is early morning, the sky blue with frothy, white clouds and there is a light breeze. She sits outside a doorway, on a step, picking apart the petals of a flower. Not a daisy, cause that really would be too much. A dandelion would do.

There is a definite sense she is waiting, for something or someone and she touches the material of her dress, as if it is somehow significant. A plain blue cardigan lies by her side, discarded. She looks up and we follow her gaze to those clouds above, as they slow race across the skyline and then back to her, her expression now changed, to one of resignation if not sadness. She reaches to her side, to the cardigan, which she picks up and wraps round her shoulders. She stands up, turns to face the door, her hand resting on the doorhandle, her other to twist the key. The door pushes open and on the threshold, on the verge of disappearing inside, she stalls, hearing in the near distance the sound of a car engine and . . .

No that's wrong, that's not what happened at all. My train of thought disturbed. I am sat on the step outside my mother's, chasing dreams. My face turned upward in search of the sun's heat, and I can hear the sound of Mr Johnson's familiar taxi, trundling slowly back up the street.

Odd, I think, what's he doing back so quick and squinting hard, I try to make out who is in the back of the cab, but dazzled by the wayward sun, I am blinded.

Glow Power Stars

Rainbow stars glow in different spectrums of colours according to a basic astronomical principle.

Stars can be hot, and they are luminous. Their surfaces burn at different temperatures:

Blue ★ 33,000°F

White ☆ 20,000°F

Violet ★ 11,000°F

Orange ★ 7,300°F

Red ★ 5,500°F

In our galaxy there is a shining object which we call the sun. The illustrating light of the sun is caused by a continuous fusion of hydrogen and helium.

The sun is the closest star at 93 million miles away.

The sun is of average brightness and size. Some stars can be a few thousand times brighter.

There are over a billion stars in our galaxy but only about 2000 can be seen in the sky.

Sometimes stars are in constellations which resemble characters and objects. Most of the names for these are from Greek and Roman mythology.

The largest star cluster is made up of super giant red stars. One of these, Antares, is 390 times larger than our sun.

White dwarfs are small stars, their size comparable to our planets.

Neutron stars are the smallest stars. Their size is only ten miles across.

All information gleaned from a packet of Glow Power Stars, including 40 colourful stars and reusable adhesive putty. Warning: choking hazard – not suitable for children under 3.